Coffee Tales

Short Stories of Wisdom

By

Sati Siroda

Book Ecke

Coffee Tales

Short Stories of Wisdom
By
Sati Siroda

Published by Book Ecke
15A, 4th Floor, City Vista, Tower A,
Suite No.1140, Fountain Road, Kharadi, Pune - 411014
Website: www.bookecke.com

ISBN
eBook: 978-81-965419-0-3
Paperback: 978-81-965419-2-7
Hardback: 978-81-965419-1-0

First edition [2023]
Adapted to American English with a New Author's Note and Introduction [2025]
Visit www.bookecke.com for any further information.

This book is dedicated to the unyielding teachings bestowed by life, shaping our paths and forging resilience within us. May this book serve as a tribute, honouring the wisdom gained through triumphs and tribulations.

BOOKS BY SATI SIRODA

Mind the Quote
Poulomi's Abode of Thoughts
Coffee Tales: Short Stories of Wisdom
Earnest Poetica: Ink Expressions of the Ineffable Heart
Gratitude Journal: Reflect, Appreciate, Transform in 60 Days
Inspiring Stories for Amazing Girls Who Believe in Themselves
Inspiring Stories for Amazing Boys Who Believe in Themselves
I Am 6 and Wonderful

Author's Note

In the grand tapestry of existence, life weaves intricate stories of joy, sorrow, love, and discovery. Within the quiet moments of contemplation, accompanied by the aromatic embrace of coffee, we find ourselves immersed in the nuances of being.

"Coffee Tales: Short Stories of Wisdom" is a humble attempt to capture these fleeting moments—where the fragility of human emotions intertwines with the comforting warmth of a cup of coffee. Each story within these pages reflects the lessons life gifts us, much like the rising steam from a freshly brewed cup, carrying whispers of resilience, growth, and understanding.

At times, this book explores *psychological themes*, including fear and uncertainty—not to unsettle, but to offer a glimpse of understanding of fear, resilience, and the light that emerges even in unsettling situations and during coping up. These elements are included to explore how hope, strength, and clarity can be found even in difficult moments. If these themes feel sensitive, please approach them with care. But if you're open to embracing both the comfort and the challenges of life, I hope these narratives offer you a fresh perspective.

So, take a moment, savor your favorite brew, and let these stories unfold. Within these pages, you may find that life—like coffee—is best enjoyed slowly, allowing its lessons seep into your heart, one sip at a time.

Yours truly,

Sati

Table of Contents

Your Free Gift

Hey There, Seeker of Stories and Wisdom!

Adulting comes with its highs and lows, but here's something to make your journey a little more exciting—**two** free e-books, just for you! Whether you need a spark of creativity, a dose of inspiration, or just a fresh perspective, these gifts are here to add a little extra spark to your day.

1. **You Got This- Mindful Reflections Journal**
- Thoughtful prompts to enrich your reading journey

2. **Mandala Coloring Book**
- A creative way to unwind and cultivate mindfulness

Scan Me

Introduction

Hey There, My Fellow Explorer of Life!

What's up?

Have you ever noticed how life's smallest moments often hold the deepest lessons? A simple conversation, a quiet observation, or even the aroma of freshly brewed coffee can spark a realization that lingers long after. That's what this book is all about—finding meaning in the everyday, wrapped in light and heartwarming stories.

This Book Is Just for You! 📖

I wrote this book because I believe in the power of **small moments and gentle wisdom**. Each story is a reflection of life's ups and downs, offering a mindful pause in your day. These aren't heavy reads; they're light, engaging, and easy to absorb—just like a good cup of your favorite brew. Whether you're taking a break, winding down for the night, or simply craving a few minutes of introspection, these stories are here to keep you company.

Why You'll Love This Book! 💚

Hey, thoughtful reader! Here's why this collection is extra special:

✔ **Bite-Sized Stories** – Perfect for a quick read during your coffee break or before bed.

✔️ **A Gentle Nudge Toward Mindfulness** – Each story offers a quiet reflection on gratitude, resilience, and self-awareness.

✔️ **A Quick Note at the End** – Every story concludes with a simple, thought-provoking takeaway to carry with you.

✔️ **A Moment Just for You** – In a fast-paced world, these stories encourage you to slow down and appreciate the beauty in the ordinary.

Are You Ready? 🚀

Let's take this journey together! Each page is filled with moments of warmth, quiet wisdom, and reflections that might just make you see life a little differently. So, grab your favorite brew, find a cozy spot, and let these stories unfold—one sip at a time.

Because, my dear reader, life—just like coffee—is best enjoyed slowly. ☕✨

With warmth and gratitude,

Sati

Chapter 1: Old Age is Inevitable

Once upon a time, a woman named Elena lived in a tiny countryside town. She had always been drawn to the peacefulness and quiet of nature and spent most of her days tending to her garden and taking long walks in the woods.

Despite her love for the outdoors, Elena had always felt a sense of unease about the future. She worried about growing old alone and often wondered if she had made the right choices in her life. As time passed, her anxiety began to take a toll on her mental health, and she found it increasingly difficult to find joy in her daily activities.

One day, Elena decided to walk through the woods to clear her mind. As she wandered through the trees, she stumbled upon a clearing she had never seen before. A large, ancient tree towered above the others in the centre of the clearing.

Without thinking, Elena approached the tree and touched its rough bark. Suddenly, she felt a rush of warmth and energy flow through her body.

It was as if the tree was speaking to her, telling her to let go of her worries and embrace the present moment.

From that day on, Elena made a conscious effort to live in the present and appreciate the beauty of her surroundings. She continued to tend to her garden and take walks in the woods, but now she did so with a renewed sense of purpose and gratitude.

As the years passed, Elena grew old but never lost her wonder and appreciation for the world around her. And when she finally passed away, she was at peace knowing she had lived a whole and meaningful life.

Quick Note

Elena's story reminds us of the significance of cherishing the present moment and discovering happiness in life's uncomplicated joys. It reminds us that worrying about the future only robs us of the beauty and serenity surrounding us. We can find contentment and create a significant life by cultivating gratitude and living purposefully.

Chapter 2: The Priceless Currency

A man named Robert lived in a bustling city filled with ambitious individuals seeking success. He was known for his exceptional integrity and unwavering moral compass. People admired his dedication toward doing the right thing, even when faced with difficult choices.

One day, as Robert walked through the crowded streets, he overheard a conversation between two businessmen. They discussed a lucrative but unethical deal that would bring them immense wealth. Intrigued, Robert couldn't resist confronting them.

"Gentlemen, forgive me for eavesdropping, but I couldn't help but overhear your conversation," Robert said politely.

The businessmen exchanged curious glances, uncertain about what to anticipate from this unfamiliar individual. Robert continued, "I implore you to reconsider your actions. While money may provide temporary comfort, it cannot buy a good reputation or inner peace."

The businessmen scoffed, dismissing Robert's words as naïveté. However, his message had struck a chord within them, planting a seed of doubt about their chosen path.

Over time, Robert's steadfast dedication to integrity and honesty garnered the respect and admiration of those in his vicinity. People sought his advice and trusted him implicitly. His reputation spread like wildfire, opening doors to opportunities he could never have imagined.

Meanwhile, the businessmen who had initially disregarded Robert's words faced the consequences of their unethical practices. Their once-thriving businesses crumbled under the weight of mistrust and negative publicity.

One day, the two businessmen approached Robert, their pride humbled and regret etched on their faces. "We should have listened to you," they admitted, their voices filled with remorse.

Robert smiled warmly, extending his hand in forgiveness. "It's never too late to make amends and rebuild your reputation. Take lessons from your

6

mistakes and opt for a different course of action. Remember, a good reputation is more valuable than any amount of money."

From that day forward, the businessmen vowed to change their ways, seeking redemption and dedicating themselves to building a reputable business based on ethical principles. As the saying goes, "Character is like a tree, and reputation its shadow."

Quick Note

The story teaches us that a good reputation holds more value than material wealth, as it is built on the foundation of character. It emphasizes prioritizing integrity and ethical values in all aspects of life. By nurturing our personality and making honourable choices, our reputation will naturally flourish, opening doors to more significant opportunities and genuine connections with others.

Chapter 3: Love Withstands All Tests

In the enchanting town of Willowbrook, two young people embarked on a captivating journey of love. Meet Rosaline, a spirited artist with a heart full of dreams, and Ethan, a brooding musician with a hidden vulnerability.

Their paths first crossed in the bustling halls of Willowbrook High School. Rosaline's vibrant sketches caught Ethan's attention, and he was drawn to how she saw the world. Each day, their encounters grew more frequent, sparking a connection neither could ignore.

As Rosaline and Ethan discovered shared passions and secrets, their bond deepened. They spent countless afternoons wandering through the town's picturesque park, exchanging heartfelt conversations amidst the whispers of falling leaves. Music became their language as Ethan strummed his guitar, and Rosaline's voice harmonized with the melody, creating a symphony of emotions.

Yet, their journey was not without obstacles. Rosaline harboured doubts about her artistic abilities, fearing she would never be good enough. Ethan struggled with his inner demons, haunted by the past. Together, they learned to support each other, finding solace and strength in their love.

Their story reached its crescendo during a moonlit evening at the annual Willowbrook Festival. Amidst twinkling fairy lights and the soft hum of laughter, Ethan took Rosaline's hand and confessed his love beneath a starry sky. Time stood still as they shared their first hug, sealing their love in pure magic.

But just as in every young love story, challenges emerged. Rosaline's dream of attending an acclaimed art school in the city threatened to pull them apart. Would they hold onto their love, despite the distance and uncertainty?

With determination and unwavering faith, Rosaline and Ethan embarked on a bittersweet journey. They navigated the trials of a long-distance relationship, each letter and phone call reinforcing their commitment. As they pursued their dreams, they discovered that love could withstand any obstacle if nurtured with patience and unwavering belief.

Years later, the room was filled with a familiar melody as the successful artist, Rosaline, showcased her breathtaking masterpieces in a prestigious gallery. Ethan, now a renowned musician, surprised her with a heartfelt serenade. In that magical moment, they both realized that their love had not only endured but had grown stronger, interweaving their passions and dreams.

Their love story, born amidst the innocent days of youth, had blossomed into a lifelong partnership. Rosaline and Ethan became a testament to the enduring power of young love, reminding us that sometimes, against all odds, love can create a masterpiece out of our lives.

Quick Note

Love can conquer distance and obstacles when nurtured with faith, support, and unwavering belief. It reminds us that pursuing our dreams doesn't mean sacrificing love but finding ways to intertwine our passions and create a beautiful symphony.

Chapter 4: Traffic Jam and the Old Lady

As I sat behind the wheel, my patience waning with each passing minute, I was trapped in a seemingly endless sea of cars. The relentless traffic jam had engulfed the road, and I was caught in the heart of it. Impatient honks and frustrated sighs filled the air as everyone around me shared the same sense of irritation and restlessness.

I glanced at the clock on my dashboard, realizing I would be late for an important meeting if the traffic didn't ease up soon. My stress levels soared as I considered the consequences of my tardiness. However, amid my frustration, I noticed a frail figure shuffling along the sidewalk.

It was an elderly woman struggling to carry a heavy bag of groceries. She appeared tired and worn out, perhaps burdened by her load and the day's scorching heat. I quickly rolled down my window and called her without a second thought.

12

"Excuse me, ma'am! Can I help you with those groceries?"

She looked up, her tired eyes filled with surprise and gratitude. With a grateful smile, she nodded, accepting my offer of assistance.

I manoeuvred my car to the side, disregarding the annoyed honks from the cars behind me. Stepping out into the blistering sun, I made my way toward her.

I gently took the heavy bag from her trembling hands as I reached her side. She sighed with relief, thanking me profusely for my kindness. We walked together, slowly but surely, as I listened to her stories of life, her grandchildren, and the challenges she faced daily.

Eventually, we reached her doorstep, where she insisted I come inside for a glass of cold water. I accepted her offer, grateful for the chance to cool down and rest momentarily. Sitting in her cosy living room, we chatted like old friends, sharing laughter and exchanging words of wisdom.

Time slipped away, and as I glanced at my watch, I realized I had spent more time with her than anticipated. I stood up with a hint of regret, thanking her for the pleasant company and expressing my desire to be on my way.

Before I left, she held my hands and looked into my eyes with genuine appreciation. "Thank you, dear," she said softly.

"Your kindness today has meant more to me than you can imagine. You've reminded me that there is still goodness in this world."

Touched by her words, I smiled warmly, realizing that in helping her, I had found a moment of respite from the frustrations of the traffic jam. As I returned to my car and merged into the flow of impatient drivers, I carried a renewed sense of compassion and a reminder of the power of a simple act of kindness.

Sati Siroda

Quick Note

The story reminds us that amidst our frustrations and busy schedules, there is always an opportunity to extend kindness and make a positive difference in someone's life. Sometimes, the smallest act of kindness can profoundly impact both the receiver and the giver, reminding us of the inherent goodness within humanity.

Chapter 5: Wired Descent

Sarah Thompson, a computer teacher at Westwood High, was excited to begin her new job. Little did she know that a sinister game was about to unfold beneath the school's facade of camaraderie.

From her first day, Sarah became the target of subtle yet persistent bullying by her fellow teachers. They mocked her skills, sabotaged her presentations, and spread malicious rumours about her. Alone and isolated, Sarah felt the weight of their cruelty pressing down on her.

But Sarah was no ordinary victim. Her passion for technology ran deep, and she had a secret weapon: her computer skills. Determined to turn the tables, she began an elaborate plan of revenge.

Using her expertise, Sarah delved into the internet's dark corners, exploring the depths of hacking and psychological manipulation. She discreetly gathered information about her tormentors, uncovering their hidden secrets and vulnerabilities.

16

As her knowledge grew, Sarah's confidence soared. With careful precision, she orchestrated a series of events that exposed the bullies, shattering their reputations and leaving them vulnerable to the judgment of their peers.

One by one, the tormentors fell into Sarah's trap. Fear consumed them as they realized they were no match for her cunning mind. The once-powerful teachers were at the mercy of the person they sought to demean.

Sarah revelled in her revenge, relishing the taste of victory. But as the torment escalated, the lines between justice and obsession blurred. The thrill of dominance twisted her mind, revealing a darkness she had never anticipated.

As the school year came to a close, Sarah's reign of terror reached its climax. The students and faculty were left in shock; their perception of right and wrong was shattered. And in the aftermath, Sarah's once-bright future was forever tainted by the price she had paid for vengeance.

Quick Note

This story serves as a chilling reminder that the line between victim and aggressor can blur as a computer teacher takes a dark journey through the realms of cyber warfare and psychological manipulation. It emphasizes that bullying can leave long-lasting and ambiguous repercussions.

Chapter 6: Kindness Unveiling Darkness

Prague, Czech Republic, 2015: One morning, Ana was startled awake by the blaring sound of her alarm clock, pulling her out of a deep slumber. The remnants of a nightmare still clung to her thoughts, leaving her unsettled. The morning sun streamed through the half-closed blinds, casting long shadows across the room. She groaned, dreading the day ahead.

As a clinical psychologist, Ana dealt with troubled minds daily. Today, she had a new patient scheduled—a man named Ethan, who had been referred to her by his family. They described him as a hermit haunted by a dark past. Ana's curiosity was piqued, but the dread within her grew with each passing moment.

Ethan arrived promptly for his session. He was tall, with messy hair and haunted eyes that seemed to carry the world's weight. His body language screamed vulnerability, but a sense of hidden danger lurked beneath the surface.

19

They began their session with the customary formalities, but it was clear that Ethan was reluctant to open up. His guarded demeanour was like a fortress, and Ana realized that unravelling his secrets would require patience and understanding. Weeks turned into months, and Ethan slowly began to trust her.

He shared fragments of his tormented past—a childhood of abuse and neglect. His traumas had shaped him into the troubled heart sitting before Ana. But as their sessions progressed, so did his healing.

One day, Ethan arrived at Ana's office visibly distressed. He trembled as he recounted a harrowing encounter on his way to their session—a confrontation with his abuser. It had shattered the fragile progress he had made. The fear in his eyes was palpable.

Ana listened intently, feeling the weight of his pain. And at that moment, she knew that she needed to show Ethan the power of kindness, not just through words but actions.

She reached out to a colleague, a detective, who agreed to investigate Ethan's claims discreetly. Meanwhile, Ana encouraged Ethan to focus on his self-care and introduced him to a support group where he could find solace among individuals who had walked a similar path.

Days turned into weeks, and with each passing session, Ana saw glimpses of hope returning to Ethan's eyes. The detective's investigation revealed evidence supporting Ethan's claims, giving him a sense of validation he had never experienced before.

During one of their final sessions, Ethan thanked Ana for all she had done. He admitted that her kindness had saved him, reminding him that compassion still existed in this often cold and unforgiving world.

As Ana bid Ethan farewell, she couldn't help but reflect on the lessons she had learned. Sometimes, the most broken hearts are the ones who need our kindness the most. Beneath the layers of pain and trauma, a spark of humanity remains, waiting to be nurtured.

From that day forward, Ana vowed to approach every patient with empathy and kindness, understanding that it could be the beacon of light that guides them out of the darkness. The most significant lesson in psychological healing is that goodwill can prevail even in the face of cruelty.

Quick Note

The story teaches us that deep wounds that need healing lie behind the guarded exteriors of troubled individuals. It reminds us of the transformative power of kindness and empathy, showing how these qualities can help someone find solace and hope in their darkest moments. Ultimately, it emphasizes the importance of approaching others with understanding and compassion, for our actions can change lives.

Chapter 7: Lost in the Dark

I'm Eliza. My adventure skills always get me into trouble! Every single time! I'll regale you with my epic trekking adventure in the forest at night today. It was a perfect recipe for a horror movie, or so I thought.

With my trusty flashlight and a backpack full of snacks (priorities, you know), I ventured into the abyss of the forest. The moon was hidden behind a thick blanket of clouds, and the only sound that accompanied me was the ominous hooting of an owl. Just the right ambience for a thrilling experience, wouldn't you agree?

As I stumbled through the darkness, my flashlight decided to play its own twisted game. First, it flickered like a dying firefly, teasing me with brief moments of illumination. Then it outright died, leaving me in pitch-black darkness. Bravo, flashlight, bravo.

Undeterred by my newfound blindness, I continued my noble quest, mindlessly stepping over every twig and rock in my path. Who needs vision, anyway? It's overrated.

Suddenly, I heard a rustling sound nearby. My heart raced faster than Usain Bolt on caffeine. Was it a ferocious predator? An ancient forest spirit? No, it was just a harmless squirrel, probably laughing at my ridiculous predicament. Thanks, Mother Nature, for the adrenaline rush.

Not one to be defeated, I summoned all my courage and relied on my impeccable sense of direction. My understanding of direction without a map in a new unexplored jungle was about as reliable as a politician's promises at that moment. I managed to navigate my way in a zig-zag motion, effectively creating my own personal labyrinth within the forest. Hooray for self-imposed challenges!

With the clock ticking and night setting in, I stumbled upon a clearing bathed in moonlight. Oh, the irony! The moon finally decided to make an appearance after I'd lost all hope. I could almost hear it chuckling, mocking my misadventures.

But wait, the hilarity doesn't end there! Just as I began to savor my triumph, I stepped into a puddle of mud the size of a small lake. If you've ever wondered what it feels like to be the star of a slapstick comedy, let me assure you, it's a muddy, squishy mess. My impeccable timing strikes again! Eventually, after hours of wandering, I emerged from the forest battered, bruised, and caked in mud from head to toe. My triumphant return to civilization was met with a mix of amusement and concern from my friends. But hey, who needs a spa day when you can experience a full-body mud treatment for free in the wilderness?

Quick Note

So, dear fellow adventurers, remember my tale of woe if you ever feel the urge to embark on a night trekking expedition in the forest. Embrace the darkness, laugh in the face of adversity, and be prepared for your flashlight to betray you. After all, life's most extraordinary adventures are often the ones that leave you questioning your sanity and covered in mud.

And duh! Carry batteries for your flashlight.

Chapter 8: Oscar's Parvo Survival

A True Story*

Thane, India, 2018: Without Oscar, our lives would have been devoid of joy and excitement. When we brought Oscar home along with Spin, who was just 45 days old, we never could have imagined the impact he would have on us. Sadly, Spin succumbed to Parvo shortly after their arrival.

It was a crisp morning in March 2018 when my mother called me, her voice filled with sorrow as she shared the heartbreaking news of Spin's passing. As tears welled in my eyes, I glanced at Oscar, my little furry companion sleeping peacefully beside the bed. Overwhelmed with grief, I held him close, and in that tender moment, he gently licked away my tears. However, the following morning, Oscar seemed lethargic and subdued, causing deep concern within me. You see, in the short time he had been with us, I had realized that Oscar was a bundle of energy wrapped in a furry coat.

Driven by fear, I rushed him to a nearby veterinary hospital named Planet Animal Hospital, anxiously locking eyes with Dr. Sarojinee and her subordinate Doctor. Deep down, I already knew what was happening, and sadly, confirmation came from my intuition. Oscar had also contracted Parvo. Dread and despair washed over both Ayush and me. With trembling voices, all I could utter was, "Please, save him!" Ayush added fervently, "We will do whatever it takes. Just save him."

Through tear-filled eyes, we braved the pain of watching Oscar receive his first intravenous (IV) treatment, praying that the capable hands of the doctors would bring him back from the brink. Every morning and evening, we sat by his side, witnessing the relentless dedication of the staff and doctors. Oscar's once lively spirit had diminished, reduced to a mere skeleton. He could hardly move, plagued by bloody vomit and loose bloody stools. The pervasive scent of IV and blood permeated our home. Yet, every time, we found solace in the unwavering presence of Dr. Sarojinee. We knew she would not let him slip away. She had promised... She had promised it herself.

At night, Ayush and I took turns sleeping while the other person cradled Oscar in their arms. Together with the doctors, Oscar fought with an indomitable spirit. He was a true hero, a tiny warrior with a stronger will to live than any of us. However, his suffering became unbearable. He stopped eating; he stopped drinking. And finally, after 11 agonizing days, on the morning of March 20th, during his routine IV drip, one of the doctors uttered the words we dreaded most, "We may have to consider putting him down. His chances of survival are tragically slim, and the pain will only increase." Numbness enveloped me as I dialled Ayush's number, his return to work cut short by the devastating news. On his way back, his desperation to be by Oscar's side was so intense that he even crashed his car into a pole.

Meanwhile, as the other doctor completed the IV, I looked hopefully at Dr. Sarojinee. At that moment, a mix of guilt and apology flashed across her expression. As I prepared to leave, she uttered the words that echoed in

28

my ears, "Let's wait for another day. If he eats, there may still be hope." She was our saving grace, our guardian angel. With her words reverberating within me, I returned home.

As soon as I gently placed Oscar on his bed, overwhelmed with emotions, I broke down. I felt utterly lost. And then, as if by a miracle, Oscar stirred, raising his left leg and leaping off the bed, crashing onto the floor. I hurried to his side, and he managed to stand up despite his weakened state.

Clutching the nutrient-rich food the doctor had prescribed, I offered it to him. With hope renewed, I opened the container, and to my joy, Oscar began to eat. He actually ate! Ayush rushed upstairs upon hearing my cries of joy, witnessing the scene of me cradling Oscar with elation. I immediately informed the doctor that Oscar had eaten, and she advised me to bring him for the evening IV, even though it had been deemed unnecessary before. With another five days of intense struggle, Oscar finally triumphed over Parvo. Though the illness had lingering effects, the doctor skillfully managed them. Our hearts are forever filled with gratitude.

Since 2018, whenever Oscar has fallen ill, I have consistently sought the expertise of Dr. Sarojinee. She is an exceptional professional, and her team is truly remarkable. Their dedication and compassion have touched our lives in immeasurable ways, forever earning our heartfelt appreciation.

Quick Note

This story underscores the profound significance of pets in our lives and highlights veterinarians' vital role in safeguarding their well-being. It imparts the importance of cherishing our animal companions and valuing veterinary professionals' devoted care. Our gratitude to Dr. Sarojinee and her team will endure indefinitely. Planet Animal Hospital has been our guiding light during every trying time we faced while caring for our little angel, Oscar.

---

*Within this chapter, "Oscar's Parvo Survival: A True Story", the author shares personal experiences, and it is essential to note that this content is devoid of any liabilities and does not constitute a promotional endorsement of any kind.

Chapter 9: Embracing the Light

Innsbruck, Austria, 2012: As I stumbled through the darkness, my heart pounded with fear. I was alone, engulfed in an inky blackness that seemed to swallow me whole. Panic began to grip my heart, its icy fingers tightening around my chest. As tears welled up in my eyes, my vision blurred even further.

But then, amid my despair, a tiny glimmer of hope flickered in the distance. A single beam of light pierced through the darkness, beckoning me forward. With trembling steps, I followed its guiding glow, clinging to the fragile thread of hope it offered.

As I drew closer, the light revealed itself as a humble candle, tenderly held by a stranger with a warm smile. "Are you lost, my dear?" she asked, her voice filled with kindness. Without hesitation, I poured out my anguish, sharing my fears and doubts.

With each word I uttered, the stranger listened intently, her eyes brimming with empathy. She understood the weight of my burdens, having carried her share of darkness in life. I felt seen, heard, and understood in her gentle presence—something I had forgotten was possible.

With a voice filled with wisdom, she spoke words that touched the depths of my wounded heart. She reminded me of the strength within me, the resilience I had forgotten I possessed. And she made me realize that even in the darkest moments, there were glimmers of light waiting to be discovered. She saved me! I wish I knew her name. But I pray, I pray for her well-being.

Gratitude blossomed within me, like a fragile flower taking root in barren soil. I was grateful for the stranger's compassion and willingness to shine her light into the abyss. But above all, I was thankful for the reminder that even in my darkest hours, there was always hope, always a way forward.

I carried her light as I bid farewell to the kind stranger and continued my journey. The darkness no longer seemed as daunting, for I knew that gratitude could illuminate even the bleakest of paths.

Quick Note

One must vow to be a candle for others—to offer warmth, guidance, and unwavering support. For in the depths of darkness, a single act of gratitude can spark a fire, lighting the way for those who have lost their light.

Chapter 10: A Haunting Night in the Old Mansion

My heart was pounding as I stood before the creaking gate of the old, abandoned mansion. The moon's eerie glow cast an ominous atmosphere over the darkened sky, shrouding the place in a haunting ambience.

The stories of haunting and torment had enticed me and my friends to this place, stirring up a mixture of excitement and unease. The air inside was thick with oppressive stillness, sending a chill down my spine. Shadows danced along the walls, their contorted forms creating unsettling shapes that seemed to taunt and tease.

My friends, Amy and Mark, stood beside me, their faces reflecting a similar mixture of fear and curiosity. We had embarked on this adventure together, seeking the thrill of the unknown. Little did we know what awaited us within these walls.

As we cautiously made our way through the darkened corridors, the silence was broken only by our footsteps echoing ominously. Each creak of the floorboards felt like a warning, as if the house knew our presence.

Low, guttural laughter suddenly echoed through the hallway, freezing us in our tracks. The laughter seemed to come from nowhere and everywhere, growing louder and more manic with each passing second. Fear clenched my heart, and I exchanged worried glances with Amy and Mark.

But then, something unexpected happened. As the laughter peaked, I noticed a hint of amusement flickering in Amy's eyes. Mark's lips twitched, and before I knew it, a giggle escaped my lips. The tension in the air seemed to dissolve as laughter erupted from each of us, growing in intensity and filling the haunted house.

We laughed uncontrollably; our fear transformed into a bizarre mixture of amusement and relief. The more we laughed, the more the house seemed to come alive, joining in our laughter riot. The portraits on the walls contorted into hilarious expressions, and even the ghostly apparitions that had haunted the mansion joined our uproarious merriment.

We stumbled through the corridors, clutching our sides and wiping tears of laughter from our eyes. The house seemed to revel in our joy as if it had been starved of human company for far too long. It was a bizarre and surreal sight; a haunted house turned into a carnival of laughter.

Hours passed, and our laughter eventually subsided, leaving us exhausted but strangely rejuvenated. As we made our way back to the entrance, we couldn't help but feel a sense of gratitude toward the house. It had turned our fears into something unexpected, bringing us together in a riot of laughter.

Leaving the haunted house, we carried the memory of that night with us, forever changed by the inexplicable joy we had found within those haunted walls. And as we looked back one last time, the house seemed to bid us farewell, a faint echo of laughter lingering in the air.

Quick Note

The haunted house taught us that sometimes the unexpected can lead to moments of joy and laughter, even amid fear. It reminded us to approach challenges with curiosity and openness, as they may hold hidden surprises. Most importantly, it emphasized the transformative power of embracing the unknown and discovering beauty in the most unlikely places.

Chapter 11: Discovering True Happiness

Once upon a time, a young girl named Margaret lived in a small village nestled between lush green hills. Despite the hardships faced by her community, Margaret was known for her radiant smile and infectious laughter. Her heart brimmed with an unwavering sense of happiness, and she seemed to spread joy wherever she went.

Margaret's days were spent exploring the beauty of nature, from the vibrant wildflowers dotting the meadows to the babbling brooks dancing through the woods. Often, she would sit under her favorite oak tree, feeling the gentle caress of the breeze on her face as she watched the clouds shape-shift across the sky.

One day, an old man named Antony, a seasoned traveller, stumbled upon the village. Intrigued by Margaret's boundless happiness, he approached her and asked, "My dear child, what's the secret behind your joyous spirit?"

Margaret warmly smiled and replied, "Sir, happiness doesn't dwell in grand treasures or distant lands. It resides within us, waiting to be uncovered. I find happiness in the simplest things—being around loved ones, savoring nature's beauty, and embracing the present moment."

Her profound wisdom stunned Antony. Despite years spent seeking happiness in material possessions and far-off places, he hadn't discovered real contentment. Intrigued by Margaret's outlook, he chose to stay in the village, hoping to unlock the mysteries of happiness.

As weeks passed, Antony observed Margaret's daily routine. He noticed her readily lending a hand to those in need, helping elderly villagers with their tasks or consoling a friend in distress. Her selflessness held the key to her happiness.

Inspired by Margaret's actions, Antony began to follow suit. He engaged with villagers, heard their tales, and offered help whenever possible. Over time, Antony realized that the more he gave, the more he received in return. The smiles, gratitude, and connections he formed brought him immense joy.

As seasons shifted and the village blossomed with newfound happiness, Antony approached Margaret again. His eyes gleamed with gratitude this time as he said, "Dear Margaret, your happiness has transformed me. I now grasp that genuine joy springs from within and flourishes when shared with others."

Margaret beamed, her eyes radiating happiness. "I'm glad, Antony. Happiness multiplies through sharing, a gift that never stops giving."

Antony and Margaret became companions from then on, traversing life together and scattering happiness wherever they journeyed. Their uncomplicated yet profound grasp of happiness changed their lives and those of everyone they encountered.

Thus, the village turned into a sanctuary of happiness, where people understood that authentic joy isn't found in pursuing material wealth but in nurturing a compassionate heart, savoring life's beauty, and bestowing the gift of happiness on others.

Quick Note

Margaret's story imparts that real happiness isn't tied to external circumstances; it's found within us through gratitude and cherishing life's simple pleasures. Acts of kindness and selflessness yield not just happiness for others but also fulfillment for ourselves. The act of sharing happiness ignites a chain reaction, reshaping our lives and fostering a harmonious, joyful community.

Chapter 12: Nature's Healing Touch

Once upon a time, a young girl named Isabella lived in a small village at the foot of a magnificent mountain. She was known for her kind heart, infectious laughter, and love for nature. Isabella spent her days exploring the lush forests, chasing butterflies, and marvelling at the vibrant flowers that painted the landscape.

One sunny morning, as Isabella ventured deeper into the woods, she stumbled upon a wounded baby deer. Its eyes were filled with fear, and it struggled to stand on its wobbly legs. Isabella's heart melted compassionately, knowing she had to help the little creature.

Gently, she cradled the deer in her arms and named it Ruby after the red gemstone that sparkled in the sunlight. With tender care, Isabella nursed Ruby back to health, feeding her and tending her wounds. The two formed an unbreakable bond, becoming inseparable companions.

As time went by, Isabella noticed that Ruby had a special gift. Whenever Ruby was near a wilting flower, her touch would revive it, bringing it back to life in all its glory. News of Ruby's miraculous ability spread throughout the village, captivating the hearts of its inhabitants.

The village, plagued by drought, desperately needed hope. The once-vibrant gardens had withered, and the people were losing faith in their ability to revive their crops. Hearing of Ruby's gift, they flocked to Isabella's doorstep, seeking her assistance.

With a heart full of empathy, Isabella and Ruby set out on a mission to restore the village's beauty. They travelled from field to field, garden to garden, and with Ruby's touch, the once-dying plants flourished once more. The habitat bloomed with abundant colors, filling the air with the sweet fragrance of flowers.

Gratitude filled the villagers' hearts, and they celebrated Isabella and Ruby's efforts with a grand feast. The village's mayor declared Isabella the official guardian of nature, and Ruby was hailed as the village's beloved mascot.

From that day forward, Isabella and Ruby continued to bring life and joy wherever they went. The village thrived, and the people learned to cherish and protect the beauty of nature. Isabella's kindness and Ruby's magical touch reminded everyone of the power of love, compassion, and the wonders nature can bestow upon those who care for it.

Thus, the tale of Isabella and Ruby turned into a legend, handed down from one generation to the next, serving as a timeless reminder for people to cherish and safeguard the world surrounding them.

Quick Note

The story teaches us that kindness and compassion can profoundly impact our world. It reminds us of the power of nurturing and caring for nature, as it has the ability to heal and bring joy. Finally, it emphasizes the importance of recognizing and embracing our unique gifts and skills, as they can be used to make a positive difference in the lives of others.

Chapter 13: Rain, Ghosts, and Laughter

Alwar, Rajasthan, 2011: I trudged through the pouring rain, my struggling umbrella attempting to shield me from the relentless downpour. The distant thunder rumbled ominously as I searched desperately for shelter. Fortunately, luck was on my side as I stumbled upon an ancient-looking palace seemingly devoured and abandoned by time.

With a mix of relief and apprehension, I approached the massive doors and pushed them open, stepping into a dimly lit hallway. The air was heavy with dust, and an eerie silence pervaded the space. It was as though the palace held its breath, waiting for something to happen.

Ignoring the voice in my head urging me to turn back, I pressed on, determined to find a haven from the storm. Room after room, I explored the deserted palace, each one filled with cobwebs and creaking floorboards. The place exuded an unsettling vibe, but I convinced myself it was merely my imagination running wild.

As I ventured deeper into the palace, the rain continued to pour outside, contributing to the eerie ambience. Suddenly, a noise reached my ears—a soft, ghostly whisper that sent a shiver down my spine. I turned around, but no one was in sight. My heart raced as I quickened my pace, eager to locate an exit.

However, fate had a different plan for me. Just as I reached what appeared to be the main hall, a gust of wind slammed the doors shut behind me, imprisoning me inside. Panic gripped me, and I frantically searched for another way out, but every exit was sealed shut. It was as though the palace intended to keep me as its unwilling guest.

To make matters worse, I heard peculiar noises— footsteps echoing through the hallways, whispers growing louder, and doors creaking open and shut on their own. I found myself trapped in a full-blown haunted house experience!

Desperate, I stumbled upon a dusty library with shelves lined with ancient books. Perhaps, within this space, I could discover something that would aid my escape from this nightmare. I selected a random book, wiping away the layer of dust that had accumulated on it.

To my astonishment, the book unveiled itself as a collection of ghost stories with illustrations of eerie spectres. I skimmed through the pages, my eyes widening with each spine-chilling tale. That's when realization struck—I needed to confront the ghosts directly. Laughter bubbled up from within me. Who would have imagined that my survival would hinge on becoming a ghostbuster?

Equipped with my newfound knowledge, I devised a plan. I gathered sheets, fastened them, and fashioned a makeshift ghost costume. I donned the comical attire and wandered through the palace, mimicking the ghostly noises I had heard earlier. To my amazement, the whispers and footsteps gradually subsided.

Soon, the palace fell silent once more. The rain had ceased, and the storm had passed. I removed the ghostly disguise, feeling both triumphant and ridiculous. It turned out that the ghosts were nothing more than mischievous spirits seeking a good laugh. And boy, did they get one!

I returned to the entrance, the grand doors now wide open, bidding me farewell. Stepping out into the fresh air, I couldn't help but chuckle at the bizarre adventure I had just undergone.

And so, with my heart still racing and a newfound respect for the supernatural, I departed from the haunted palace, forever grateful for the rain that had led me to that hilariously haunted encounter. I'm still attempting to decipher what lay within and what transpired. I have yet to return. Once was evidently sufficient, I suppose.

Quick Note

Sometimes, we stumble upon unexpected and eerie experiences. While fear and uncertainty are natural, confronting our fears head-on is crucial. Embracing a sense of humour and devising creative solutions can assist us in overcoming challenges, transforming seemingly haunting situations into unforgettable adventures.

Chapter 14: Unleashing Joyful Hearts

In the heart of a lush, vibrant jungle, there lived a curious and adventurous monkey named Kiki. Kiki swung through the trees, his laughter echoing through the canopy as he explored every nook and cranny of his enchanting home. He was content and filled with boundless energy, but deep inside, he yearned for something more—true happiness.

One sunny morning, as Kiki leapt from branch to branch, he stumbled upon an ancient, wise parrot named Roto. Roto had travelled far and wide, gathering wisdom from different corners of the world. Intrigued by the parrot's colorful feathers and sagacious gaze, Kiki approached him, his eyes sparkling with curiosity.

"Roto," Kiki called out, "I've been searching for happiness in this jungle, but I can't find it. Can you show me the way?"

Roto cocked his head, studying Kiki briefly before his beak curled into a knowing smile. "Kiki, my dear friend," he said, "happiness is not something you find; it's something you create within yourself and share with others. Let me show you."

With great enthusiasm, Roto guided Kiki deeper into the jungle, away from the familiar paths he had explored countless times. They encountered a family of playful monkeys leaping and frolicking in a clearing. Kiki watched them; his heart filled with joy as their laughter intertwined with the rustling leaves.

"Look, Kiki," Roto whispered, "happiness often lies in the connections we forge with others. These monkeys find happiness in their togetherness, love, and laughter."

Eager to experience that kind of happiness, Kiki joined the playful monkeys. He swung from tree to tree, laughing and embracing the shared camaraderie. In their company, Kiki felt a sense of belonging and a warmth that filled his heart.

As they continued their journey, Roto led Kiki to a serene waterfall, its crystal-clear waters cascading into a glistening pool. Nearby, a wise old turtle basked in the sun, her eyes sparkling with wisdom.

"Kiki," the turtle began, "happiness is also found in appreciating the beauty of nature and finding peace within ourselves. Look around you, and you'll see the wonders surrounding us."

In the presence of the tranquil waterfall, Kiki sat by the water's edge, watching the vibrant butterflies flutter and the colorful flowers sway. He closed his eyes, allowing the gentle sounds and scents of the jungle to wash over him. He felt a profound sense of peace and harmony in that moment of stillness.

As Kiki and Roto continued their journey, they stumbled upon a clearing where animals of different species coexisted peacefully. The lion rested next to the gazelle, the monkey shared a branch with a colorful parrot, and the snake wound through the grass, unmindful of the others. They all lived in harmony, appreciating the diversity and uniqueness of their companions.

"Roto," Kiki whispered in awe, "this unity, this acceptance—it's beautiful. Is this where happiness resides?"

Roto nodded, his eyes gleaming with pride. "Indeed, Kiki. True happiness can be found in embracing diversity, accepting one another, and living in harmony. In this jungle, all creatures celebrate their differences and find joy in the connections they form."

As days turned into weeks, Kiki embraced the wisdom Roto shared. He continued to explore the jungle, but now with a renewed perspective. He sought connections with others, appreciated the beauty of his surroundings, and embraced the diversity surrounding him.

Quick Note

True happiness is not something we find externally but create within ourselves. It can be found in forming genuine connections with others, appreciating the beauty of nature, and embracing diversity. We can unlock the key to lasting happiness by seeking joy in these aspects.

Chapter 15: Journey to Happiness

Once upon a time, a young woman named Rosaline lived in a quaint town. Despite the comfort and stability of her life, she yearned for something more. Deep within her was a fire, a burning desire to truly live and be happy.

Rosaline embarked on a journey of self-discovery, determined to uncover the secrets to genuine happiness and fulfill her aspirations. She began by embracing her authenticity, accepting herself fully, flaws and all. No longer afraid of judgment, she embraced her uniqueness and allowed her true self to shine.

Next, Rosaline delved into her passions. She spent hours painting, losing herself in vibrant colors and strokes of creativity. With each brushstroke, she felt a sense of fulfillment and joy she had never experienced. Pursuing her passions became a non-negotiable part of her daily life.

Gratitude became Rosaline's daily practice. She made a habit of counting her blessings, appreciating the small wonders that surrounded her. From the chirping birds outside her window to the warm embrace of loved ones, she found solace in acknowledging the beauty in each moment.

Rosaline understood the power of nurturing relationships. She reached out to old friends and forged new connections. Surrounding herself with positive and supportive individuals, she created a community that uplifted her spirits and inspired her to keep moving forward.

Finally, Rosaline adopted a growth mindset. She saw setbacks and challenges as opportunities for learning and growth. Instead of being discouraged by failures, she embraced them as stepping stones toward her aspirations.

As time passed, Rosaline's life blossomed. She radiated happiness, her infectious energy touching the lives of those around her. She became an inspiration to others, proof that genuine happiness was attainable.

People sought her out, eager to know her secret. With a smile, Rosaline shared her wisdom: "To be truly happy and live your aspirations, be true to yourself, follow your passions, cherish the blessings, nurture relationships, and embrace the lessons life offers."

And so, the story of Rosaline spread far and wide, reminding all that happiness is not a distant dream but a journey within reach. Rosaline had changed the town forever, and her legacy of joy and fulfillment touched lives for generations to come.

Quick Note

To be truly happy and live your aspirations, embrace authenticity, pursue passions, cultivate gratitude, nurture relationships, and embrace a growth mindset.

Chapter 16: Fear Conquered

Awoman named Lucinda lived in the small town of Oakridge, nestled amidst the towering mountains. Her life had been sheltered, wrapped in the safety of routines. But fate had a different plan in store.

One stormy night, a bone-chilling experience shook Lucinda's world. A sudden landslide trapped her within the confines of her own home. Fear gripped her heart as she realized she was alone, cut off from the outside world.

Days turned into weeks as she awaited rescue. With each passing moment, Lucinda felt the weight of uncertainty pressing upon her. But within the depths of despair, a flicker of resilience ignited. She knew she had to take charge of her fate.

Driven by necessity, Lucinda adapted. She scavenged for food, relying on her wit and resourcefulness to survive. She braved the treacherous landscape outside her doorstep, searching for hope amidst the devastation. With each obstacle overcome, her strength grew.

As the days turned into months, Lucinda's transformation became evident. The timid woman who once feared change now embraced it. She discovered her abilities, unearthing a wellspring of courage deep within her.

Through the isolation, Lucinda found solace in the books that lined her shelves. She devoured stories of triumph over adversity, drawing inspiration from the characters who faced their demons. The words breathed life into her spirit, reminding her she possessed the power to overcome.

Finally, the day arrived when rescue teams reached her home. But Lucinda was no longer the same person they expected to find. She emerged from her self-imposed prison, not as a victim, but as a woman reborn.

Her experience had taught her that life's challenges were not to be feared but embraced. She had learned the value of self-reliance and the depths of her resilience. As she stepped into the sunlight, Lucinda vowed to live her life with a newfound purpose and the unwavering belief that she could conquer anything that came her way.

From that day forward, Lucinda became a beacon of hope for others, sharing her story of transformation and inspiring those who felt trapped by their circumstances. They saw a reflection of their strength waiting to be unleashed in her.

And so, in the wake of that bone-chilling experience, Lucinda became a living testament to the indomitable spirit of the human heart.

Quick Note

The story reminds us that despite adversity, we have untapped reservoirs of strength waiting to be discovered. It teaches us that embracing challenges can lead to personal growth and transformation. Ultimately, it underscores the importance of self-belief and the power of resilience in navigating life's obstacles.

Chapter 17: Notes, Paranoia, and Laughter

I woke up one morning feeling dizzy and disoriented. As I stumbled into the kitchen, I noticed a peculiar note on the refrigerator that read, "I know what you did. Don't try to run." My heart skipped a beat, and I looked around, expecting someone to jump out and yell, "Surprise!" But the house was eerily silent, and I couldn't shake off the feeling that someone was watching me.

I brushed it off as a silly prank and continued my day, ignoring the nagging paranoia slowly creeping in. However, as the days passed, the notes appeared randomly: on the bathroom mirror, under my pillow, and even taped to my car's windshield. Each message was more menacing than the last, and they seemed to know intimate details about my life. I couldn't understand who could be playing such a twisted game with me. Was it a friend, a foe, or a deranged squirrel with a penchant for practical jokes?

My mind spun with possibilities, and I started questioning everyone I knew. My best friend, Tom, denied involvement and suggested I seek professional help. He handed me a business card for a psychologist named Dr. Hill.

Dr. Hill was known for his unorthodox methods, but I was desperate for answers. I made an appointment and arrived at his office, which resembled a clown's secret lair with its walls adorned with bright colors and humorous posters.

Dr. Hill, a tall man with wild curly hair and a polka-dotted suit, welcomed me with a broad smile. "Ah, my dear patient, welcome to the Carnival of the Mind!" he exclaimed, twirling a fake flower on his lapel. I told him about the mysterious notes and my growing paranoia. Instead of offering comforting words, he burst into laughter – a maniacal laugh that echoed through the room. I felt a chill run down my spine, unsure whether this was a good idea.

After a few minutes of uncontrollable laughter, Dr. Hill composed himself and wiped tears of joy from his eyes.

"You, my friend, are a victim of the ultimate prank," he finally said, grinning from ear to ear. My eyes widened in disbelief. "A prank? But who would go to such lengths?" Dr. Hill explained that Tom had been behind it all, orchestrating the elaborate scheme to teach me a lesson about taking life too seriously. He believed that laughter was the ultimate therapy and that my paranoia resulted from my overly analytical mind.

Relief and frustration washed over me simultaneously. I couldn't decide whether to go and hug Tom or strangle him. Ultimately, I settled for a weak smile, realizing I had been the unwitting star of a darkly comedic psychological thriller. From that day forward, I learned to embrace the absurdity of life. And though I moved on, I hid all the sticky notes and prank props in case revenge was ever on my mind. After all, laughter might be therapeutic, but a harmless prank now and then couldn't hurt either.

Quick Note

The story highlights the importance of not taking life too seriously and embracing the absurdity of unexpected situations. It teaches us that laughter can be a powerful tool for therapy and overcoming our anxieties. Ultimately, it reminds us to balance analyzing life's challenges and finding humour in the unexpected.

Chapter 18: The Haunting Within

I woke up in a dimly lit room, disoriented and unable to recall how I got there. Shadows danced ominously on the walls, and a cold breeze whispered through the cracks. Panic gripped my chest, squeezing tighter with every breath.

A barely audible voice slithered into my ears: "Welcome to your nightmare." It echoed, sending shivers down my spine.

I stumbled forward, seeking an escape from this claustrophobic prison. However, with each step, the walls seemed to close in, suffocating me. The air grew heavier, laced with a scent of decay and despair.

As I explored further, I discovered photographs scattered across the floor. My heart pounded as I recognized the faces—friends, family, loved ones—all wearing expressions of terror and anguish. Trembling, I reached out to touch one, only to have it crumble to dust in my hands.

Whispers grew louder, hissing into my mind, revealing secrets deep within my subconscious. Memories flooded back, distorted and fragmented, twisting my perception of reality. I struggled to distinguish between what was real and what was a fabrication of my mind.

A mirror, cracked and tarnished, caught my reflection. My eyes once filled with innocence, now mirrored a chilling emptiness. A sinister grin spread across my face, involuntary and unnatural.

I then realized that the room was not merely a prison but a manifestation of my guilt and darkest fears. It had become a twisted playground, tormenting my sanity.

A voice whispered again, closer this time, "You can never escape your mind." And at that moment, the room swallowed me whole, trapping me in an eternal nightmare of my creation.

Quick Note

This short story serves as a chilling reminder of the power of our minds and the depths of our fears. It highlights the importance of confronting our inner demons and facing our past traumas rather than allowing them to consume us. Ultimately, it teaches that liberating ourselves from our minds demands courage, self-reflection, and a readiness to confront the deepest corners of our psyche.

Chapter 19: Better or Bitter

In a small coastal town lived a young woman named Lilith. She had faced her fair share of challenges and setbacks but refused to let them define her. One day, while sitting on a bench overlooking the sea, Lilith noticed an elderly man approaching her with a gentle smile.

"Good day, young lady," he greeted warmly. "May I join you for a moment?"

Lilith nodded, curious about the stranger's intentions. "Of course, please have a seat."

The man settled on the bench, his wise eyes filled with serenity. "I couldn't help but notice the strength in your eyes despite the trials life may have thrown your way. Tell me, what is your secret?"

Lilith contemplated his words momentarily before responding, "I believe that no matter the circumstance, we always have a choice in how we respond. We can let bitterness consume us or use our experiences to grow stronger and better."

The man nodded, his silver hair shimmering in the sunlight. "Ah, the power of choice. It truly is a remarkable gift we possess. My dear, our circumstances may be beyond our control, but our attitude and actions are entirely up to us."

Lilith looked at the crashing waves, a newfound sense of clarity washing over her. "I've learned that dwelling on the negative and allowing bitterness to take root only holds me back. Instead, I focus on what I can do to overcome challenges and create a better future."

The man smiled, his eyes twinkling with wisdom. "Indeed, my dear. Life may not always go as planned, but our true character is revealed in those moments of adversity. We can either let circumstances define us or rise above them, becoming the best version of ourselves."

Lilith took a deep breath, feeling a renewed sense of empowerment. "Thank you for reminding me of the power of choice. I will strive to embrace a positive attitude and take charge of my destiny."

The man stood up, his presence radiating tranquillity. "Remember, my dear, you have the ability to shape your path. The choice is always yours. May you continue to grow stronger and better, no matter what life brings."

With those parting words, the man walked away, leaving Lilith inspired and determined to live by his shared wisdom. From that day forward, she embraced each challenge as an opportunity for growth, choosing to become better rather than bitter. As she faced life's ups and downs, Lilith carried the lesson of choice, constantly reminding herself that no matter the circumstance, she held the power to shape her attitude and create the desired results.

Quick Note

This story teaches us that our attitude and response to circumstances are within our control. We have the power to choose whether we become bitter or better due to our experiences. Embracing a positive attitude and taking responsibility for our actions can lead to personal growth and a better future.

Chapter 20: Subterranean Shadows

In the heart of a bustling city, amidst the echoing tunnels, a woman found herself trapped in a desolate subway station. It was late at night, and the last train had departed. Panic gripped her as the flickering lights cast eerie shadows on the cold, tiled walls.

As the minutes turned into hours, her mind began to unravel. Whispers echoed through the abandoned platform, playing tricks on her sanity. She sensed an unseen presence lurking in the darkness, watching her every move.

She reached for her phone with trembling hands and found no signal. She was isolated, cut off from the world above. Fear consumed her as she imagined the worst: an unknown danger lurking nearby, waiting to pounce.

Time stretched on, and desperation settled in. She ventured deeper into the labyrinth of tunnels, her footsteps echoing hauntingly. As she wandered, strange sounds filled the air—distant cries, echoing laughter, and whispers that seemed to come from within the very walls themselves.

Every turn revealed nothing but more darkness and uncertainty. Her heart pounded as she felt a chilling presence closing in. Shadows danced and merged, taking sinister forms in her imagination. Paranoia wrapped its icy fingers around her, eroding her sanity.

Just as hope was fading, a faint glimmer of light appeared ahead. She hurried toward it, her breath catching in her throat. As she emerged from the subway's depths, the bustling city greeted her with open arms. She gasped for air, the weight of the night's terrors lifting from her shoulders.

Though she had escaped the confines of the subway, the haunting memories would forever remain etched in her mind. The experience had changed her, leaving a residue of unease and an unshakable realisation that darkness can lurk even in the most mundane places.

Quick Note

The story highlights the fragility of our sense of safety and control in unfamiliar and isolated environments. It reminds us to trust our instincts and remain vigilant in uncertain situations. Additionally, it explores the depths of our fears and the resilience we can find within ourselves when faced with adversity.

Chapter 21: Muddy Heroics

Thembang, Arunachal Pradesh, India: One sunny day, we drove through the breathtaking mountainous terrain when something extraordinary caught Ocii's attention.

As we cruised in my trusty car, the wind blowing through the open windows, Ocii suddenly started barking excitedly. His tail wagged furiously, and I couldn't help but wonder what had gotten him so riled up.

"What is it, Ocii?" I asked, glancing at him curiously.

With his doggy eyes sparkling, Ocii pointed his nose toward a muddy pit up ahead. My eyes widened with surprise as I spotted a horse trapped and struggling to free itself. I could sense the urgency in Ocii's barks as he urged me to halt the car.

"Stop the car, Momma! We've got to help that horse!" Ocii barked insistently.

Without a second thought, I pulled the car to a stop. I couldn't believe what I was seeing. There, in front of us,

73

was a horse needing our assistance. I felt a surge of determination rising within me.

Ocii and I quickly grabbed a rope from the trunk and approached the horse. Its eyes seemed to plead for help, and I knew we had to act fast.

"Don't worry, big guy! We're here to save you," I reassured the horse as Ocii wagged his tail in agreement.

Ocii and I carefully worked together to tie the rope around the horse's body, ensuring it was secure. We attached the other end of the string to the car, ready to give our new friend the tug it needed.

With a deep breath, I started the engine, and slowly but surely, the car began to pull. With every pull, the car's tires spun in the thick mud, leaving deep tracks in their wake. The once spotless vehicle now wore a coat of dirt, proudly displaying the evidence of our daring rescue mission. Mud splattered everywhere, and we couldn't help but laugh as the car slipped and slid in the muck. It was quite a sight, but we were determined to free the horse.

After what felt like an eternity but was probably only a few minutes, the horse finally found solid ground. Covered in mud from head to hoof, he stood tall and proud, giving us a grateful neigh. It was as if he was saying, "Thank you, guys!"

Ocii and I exchanged looks, our muddy appearance only making us laugh even harder. We had succeeded in our mission, and the joy that filled our hearts was immeasurable.

With a final pat on the horse's back, we bid him farewell and continued our journey. We may have been a mess, but we didn't mind. We had made a difference, and that was all that mattered.

And so, my friends, that's how Ocii and I turned a muddy mishap into a victorious rescue. It taught us that even in messy situations, we can achieve incredible things when we work together with love and determination.

Quick Note

This muddy adventure taught us that sometimes, helping others means getting a little dirty ourselves, but the joy of making a difference outweighs any discomfort. We learned the power of teamwork and determination. Ocii and I overcame the challenges and successfully rescued the trapped horse. The experience reminded us that even in the most unexpected situations, we can create remarkable and heartwarming stories of compassion and heroism when we follow our instincts and act kindly.

Chapter 22: The Rescuer and Protector

O nce upon a time, in a small town nestled among rolling hills, there lived a kind-hearted little girl named Ellie. Ellie had a heart full of compassion for all living creatures and a special love for animals. She spent her days exploring the woods and fields, always on the lookout for a new friend.

One sunny day, as Ellie wandered near a meadow, she heard a faint whimpering sound. She followed the sound until she stumbled upon a tiny, shivering puppy hiding beneath a bush. The poor creature had gotten separated from its mother and desperately needed help.

Ellie scooped up the puppy and cradled it without a second thought. She could see the fear and sadness in its eyes and knew she couldn't leave it behind. Determined to save the little pup, she brought it home, much to the delight of her family.

Ellie named her new companion Oliver and devoted herself to his care. She fed him, bathed him, and cuddled with him. They became inseparable friends, and their bond grew stronger each day. Grateful for Ellie's love and kindness, Oliver would wag his tail and shower her with puppy kisses.

Years went by, and Ellie and Oliver grew up together. They shared countless adventures and cherished memories. Oliver had transformed from a fragile puppy into a loyal and protective dog, always by Ellie's side. He had become her best friend, her confidant, and her guardian.

One stormy night, as Ellie slept soundly in her room, a fire broke out in the house. Smoke filled the air, and the flames engulfed everything in their path. Ellie awoke to the sound of the crackling fire, terrified and disoriented. Coughing and gasping for air, she stumbled out of bed, but the thick smoke made it nearly impossible to find her way.

Suddenly, through the chaos and panic, Oliver's barks pierced the air. Guided by his unwavering loyalty, Ellie followed his voice through the darkness and smoke. She could hear him scratching and pawing at the door. With renewed hope, Ellie pushed open the door, and fresh air rushed in, providing a lifeline amidst the suffocating fumes.

Together, Ellie and Oliver made their way out of the burning house, their hearts pounding with fear and relief. The firefighters arrived just in time to extinguish the flames and ensure their safety. As Ellie clung to Oliver, tears streaming down her face, she realised the little puppy she had once rescued had now saved her life.

From that day forward, the bond between Ellie and Oliver deepened even more. They were a living testament to the power of love, compassion, and the unbreakable connection between humans and animals. Their story spread throughout the town, inspiring others to cherish and protect all creatures, great and small. And so, in that small town where kindness bloomed and hearts were touched, Ellie and Oliver lived a life filled with love, gratitude, and the joy of knowing they had each other forever.

Quick Note

The story of Ellie and Oliver teaches us the profound impact that compassion and kindness can have on the lives of others, including animals. It reminds us to be attentive to the needs of those around us, regardless of their size or species. Furthermore, it highlights the importance of nurturing and cherishing the bonds we form, as they can provide us with unwavering support and even save our lives in times of adversity.

Chapter 23: Breaking Free from Hesitation

In a small town nestled among rolling hills, two friends, Alex and Emily, sat on a park bench, enjoying the warm summer breeze.

Alex sighed deeply, gazing into the distance. "You know, Emily, I've always admired those who dare to seize the day."

Emily looked at Alex with curiosity. "What do you mean?"

"We often hesitate when we should act," Alex explained. "We let fear and self-doubt hold us back from pursuing our dreams and taking risks."

Emily nodded thoughtfully. "You're right. We often wonder what could have been if we had just taken that leap of faith."

"Exactly!" Alex exclaimed. "There's an old proverb that says 'Carpe Diem—seize the day.' It's a reminder that we should never hesitate when the time comes to act."

Emily pondered for a moment. "But why do we hesitate? Is it because we're afraid of failure?"

Alex nodded. "Fear of failure, lack of confidence, and the unknown can paralyse us. But the truth is, we're imprisoning ourselves in a cage of missed opportunities by not taking action."

A determined look appeared on Emily's face. "So, what should we do, Alex? How can we break free from this hesitation?"

"We need to embrace the mindset of seizing the day," Alex replied. "Whenever we feel it's time to act, we must summon the courage to take that leap. Even if we stumble or face setbacks, we'll gain wisdom and grow in the process."

Emily smiled. "You're right. We'll never know what could happen unless we try. Let's make a pact, Alex, to seize the day from now on."

Alex extended a hand, and they shook hands on their pact. "Absolutely, Emily! Let's not let hesitation hold us back anymore. We'll take action and embrace every opportunity that comes our way."

From that day forward, Alex and Emily lived by their pact. They pursued their passions, faced challenges head-on, and refused to let hesitation hinder their progress. And as they embraced the mantra of "Carpe diem," they discovered a world of possibilities that they had once thought were beyond their reach.

Through their actions, they inspired others, showing them the power of not hesitating when the time to act arises. And as they seized each day with unwavering determination, they found fulfillment and happiness, knowing they had lived life to the fullest.

Quick Note

The story teaches us that hesitation can hold us back from pursuing our dreams and taking risks. By embracing the mindset of seizing the day and acting, we open ourselves up to new opportunities and growth. Even amidst stumbling or encountering setbacks, the invaluable experience gained from unwavering determination paves the way for profound wisdom and transformative personal growth.

Chapter 24: The Journey of Knowledge and Creation

O nce upon a time, a young and passionate painter named Laura lived in a quaint town filled with artists. Her deep knowledge of painting techniques, art history, and color theory was unparalleled. She could spend hours discussing the intricacies of renowned artists' works and their impact on the art world. However, despite her vast knowledge, Laura had yet to experience the sheer joy and fulfillment of practising her skills.

One sunny morning, Laura's eyes lit up excitedly as she strolled through a local art gallery. A flyer caught her attention—an upcoming exhibition presenting the works of emerging artists. This serendipitous event was the perfect opportunity for Laura to transcend the confines of theoretical understanding and venture into the realm of creative expression.

With unwavering determination, Laura set up her easel and gathered her brushes and paints. As she stood before the blank canvas, anticipation and nervousness coursed through her veins. Doubts whispered in her ear, questioning her ability to bring her knowledge to life. But deep down, she knew that this was her moment—to experience what she had learned and to let her artistic spirit soar.

With a deep breath, Laura dipped her brush into vibrant hues and made her first strokes on the canvas. The colors danced across the surface, blending and evolving with each delicate movement of her hand. In that sacred space between brush and canvas, Laura discovered the true essence of her art—a unique fusion of knowledge and personal expression.

Days turned into weeks as Laura poured her mind and heart onto the canvas. Every stroke, every layer of paint, carried the weight of her dedication and newfound understanding. She confronted challenges head-on, learning to embrace imperfections as opportunities for growth. Through the process, Laura experienced first-hand the transformation that occurs when knowledge meets action.

Finally, the day of the exhibition arrived. The gallery walls were adorned with vibrant works of art, each bearing the heart of its creator. Amidst the buzzing crowd, Laura's painting stood proudly, a testament to her journey of self-discovery.

Visitors gravitated toward Laura's artwork, captivated by its emotional depth. They marvelled at her ability to weave her extensive knowledge into a tangible masterpiece seamlessly. With each admiring gaze and every word of praise, Laura felt an overwhelming sense of fulfillment—her art had transcended the realm of theory, becoming an extension of her very being.

From that day forward, Laura's perspective shifted. She understood that actual artistic growth lies not only in knowledge but also in the act of creation. She continued to expand her understanding, always seeking new techniques and inspirations, but now armed with the wisdom that experience brings. Laura became a beacon of inspiration for aspiring artists, reminding them to immerse themselves fully in the art they loved and to never shy away from experiencing what they had learned.

And so, Laura's artistic journey continued, guided by the timeless truth that no matter how much one knows, true mastery and personal fulfillment are attained through the act of doing.

Quick Note

The story of Laura reminds us of the importance of putting knowledge into action. More than merely possessing theoretical understanding is required; we must immerse ourselves in the practical application to truly grasp its depth. Through her journey, Laura discovers the transformative power of experience, embracing imperfections and allowing her art to become an extension of her being.

Chapter 25: The Path to a Good Life

O nce upon a time, a young woman named Anastasia lived in a bustling city filled with dreams and aspirations. She had a burning desire for a good life filled with success, emotional fulfillment, and meaningful connections. However, Anastasia soon learned that good things don't come quickly.

As she embarked on her journey, Anastasia encountered numerous hurdles and challenges. It became clear to her that luck could only take her so far. She realized the path to a fulfilling life required relentless effort, resilience, and the willingness to learn from her mistakes.

One evening, as Anastasia sat with her wise mentor, Mr. Roberts, she expressed her frustrations. "Mr. Roberts, it feels like a never-ending battle. I've been working tirelessly, but the results seem so elusive."

Mr. Roberts, with a knowing smile, leaned forward and said, "Anastasia, my dear, remember that good things rarely come without a fight. You'll achieve the life you desire through your unwavering determination and the ability to persevere."

Anastasia pondered his words. "But what if someone else could fight my battles for me? Would that not make the journey easier?"

Mr. Roberts chuckled gently. "Anastasia, though we may indeed receive support and encouragement from others, no one can fight our battles with the same vigour and devotion as we would. Your dreams, aspirations, and desire for a good life reside within you. It is your responsibility to pursue them with passion and unwavering dedication."

Anastasia realized the truth in his words. She understood that relying solely on luck or expecting others to pave the way would only lead to disappointment. She had to take ownership of her journey and be willing to invest her time, energy, and effort to shape her destiny.

From that moment forward, Anastasia embraced the challenges that came her way. She tackled them head-on, viewing each setback as an opportunity for growth.

She dedicated herself to honing her skills, expanding her knowledge, and fostering meaningful connections.

Over time, Anastasia's perseverance paid off. Her career blossomed, and she discovered the emotional satisfaction she had longed for. She forged genuine friendships based on trust and mutual support along the way.

As Anastasia reflected on her journey, she realized the struggle was integral to her success. Through the hardships and her unwavering commitment, she built a life worth cherishing.

Quick Note

Anastasia's journey teaches us that good things require hard work and dedication. Luck can only take us somewhat far, but our efforts determine our success and fulfillment. By taking ownership of our path, learning from our mistakes, and persisting through challenges, we have the power to shape a life worth cherishing.

Chapter 26: A Wake-Up Call

O nce upon a time, a spirited young man named Ethan lived in a vibrant city filled with youthful exuberance. He revelled in the thrill of late-night parties, indulging in unhealthy habits without a care in the world. To him, his invincible youth seemed like an impenetrable shield protecting him from any consequences.

One fateful day, Ethan felt an unexpected pain in his chest while enjoying a carefree evening with friends. It took his breath away, leaving him in a state of shock. Fear gripped his heart as he realized his reckless lifestyle might have caught up with him.

Determined to find answers and seek guidance, Ethan scheduled an appointment with Dr. Anderson, a wise and experienced physician. Sitting in the doctor's office, anxiety coursing through his veins, Ethan poured out his concerns.

Dr. Anderson listened attentively, his eyes filled with empathy. "Ethan, my young friend, it's true that when

92

we're young, we often believe we're invincible. But the truth is, our choices today can profoundly impact our future health."

Ethan nodded, his face reflecting a mix of regret and realization. "I never thought about the consequences of my actions. I thought I had all the time in the world to care for my health."

Dr. Anderson smiled warmly. "It's never too late to start, Ethan. But taking care of your health early can make a significant difference. By developing healthy habits now, you can prevent future problems and pave the way for a fulfilling and vibrant future."

Ethan sighed, contemplating the doctor's words. "What should I do, Dr. Anderson? How can I turn things around?"

The physician leaned forward, his voice filled with gentle wisdom. "Start by making small changes, Ethan. Incorporate nutritious foods into your diet, exercise regularly, and prioritize quality sleep. Make sure to schedule regular check-ups with both your doctor and dentist. This will help you monitor your health and address any potential issues before they can worsen."

Ethan nodded, a newfound determination lighting up his eyes. He realized that caring for his health was not a burden but a gift he needed to embrace. With each passing day, he committed himself to making healthier choices, one step at a time.

As the years passed, Ethan reaped the rewards of his newfound commitment to his well-being. His body and mind grew more robust, allowing him to vigorously pursue his passions and dreams. He saw his friends facing health challenges and realized that the choices he had made early on had indeed shaped his future.

Ethan became an advocate for prioritizing health, sharing his story, and inspiring others to make positive changes in their lives. Through his experiences, he learned that it's never too early to start caring for one's health, as each choice made today can lay the foundation for a fulfilling and vibrant future.

Sati Siroda

Quick Note

The story of Ethan reminds us of the importance of prioritizing our health from a young age. Neglecting our well-being in our youth can have long-term consequences. By developing healthy habits early, seeking regular check-ups, and making positive choices, we can lay the foundation for a vibrant and fulfilling future.

Chapter 27: Embracing the Essence of Every Moment

A young woman named Eva resided in a picturesque town nestled among rolling hills and adorned with vibrant flowers. She revelled in the carefree days of her twenties, cherishing the endless possibilities ahead. However, little did she know that life's fleeting nature would soon impart a valuable lesson.

One sunny afternoon, Eva sat on a park bench, gazing at children playing and the bustling world; a sense of nostalgia washed over her. She realized that time was slipping through her fingers like grains of sand. With newfound urgency, she vowed to make every moment count.

She embarked on a journey of seizing the day, embracing the essence of each passing moment. Relentlessly, she pursued her passions, cherishing the youthful energy fuelling her dreams. Every day became a canvas waiting to be painted with vibrant hues of experience and memory.

During a serendipitous encounter at a local café, Eva conversed with an elderly gentleman named Mr. Evans. They discussed life's fleeting nature, and Mr. Evans shared his regrets of not fully embracing his youth and the opportunities that came with it.

Eva listened intently, her heart filled with determination and trepidation. "But is it ever too late, Mr. Evans? Can we still make a difference even if we've missed some things?"

Mr. Evans smiled, a twinkle in his eyes. "My dear Eva, life is short, but each moment is a chance for renewal and growth. It's never too late to pursue what brings you joy and fulfillment. The key is to live fully in the present, appreciating every breath and making the most of the time you have."

Inspired by Mr. Evans' wisdom, Eva embarked on a mission to embrace the present moment. She immersed herself in the beauty of nature, pursued her artistic passions, and nurtured deep connections with loved ones. The simple act of savoring a cup of coffee became a mindful meditation, reminding her to cherish even the most minor pleasures.

With each passing day, Eva experienced a newfound zest for life. She revelled in the laughter of friends, danced in the rain, and relished the taste of adventure. The worries and anxieties that once held her back faded into insignificance as she embraced the fleeting nature of time.

As the years went by, Eva reflected on her journey with gratitude. She realized that life indeed flew by faster than anyone could imagine. However, embracing every moment's essence, she transformed her life into a tapestry woven with vibrant memories and meaningful experiences.

Quick Note

The story of Eva teaches us the significance of cherishing every moment. Life passes swiftly, and we must make the most of our time. Living fully in the present, embracing opportunities, and nurturing meaningful connections can create a life enriched with joy, fulfillment, and cherished memories.

Chapter 28: Harmony in Acceptance

A wise old man named Samuel lived in a peaceful village nestled amidst lush greenery. He had learned through the ups and downs of life that sometimes, the best way to navigate relationships and avoid unnecessary conflicts was to live and let live. One sunny afternoon, as Samuel sat in the shade of a towering oak tree, a young woman named Sarah approached him with an eager expression. "Samuel, I can't help but notice that James is making a big mistake. I feel the need to intervene and show him the right path."

Samuel smiled kindly, his eyes reflecting a lifetime of wisdom. "Sarah, my dear, remember that each person's journey is unique. While your intentions may be pure, interfering without being sought can create misunderstandings and strain relationships. Sometimes, it's best to let others seek guidance when ready." Sarah frowned as her desire to help was still evident. "But what if I know I can make a positive impact? Shouldn't I try to prevent him from making a mistake?"

Samuel gently placed a hand on her shoulder. "It is commendable to wish to help others, Sarah, but forcing our ideas onto them can create resistance. Instead, be a beacon of light, living your life in a way that inspires and invites others to seek your guidance when they are open to it. Respect their journeys and trust that they will find their path, even if it includes making mistakes."

As Sarah absorbed Samuel's words, she realized the truth in his wisdom. She understood that trying to control others' choices often led to unintended consequences and strained relationships. She vowed to adopt a new perspective—living authentically and trusting that those who needed guidance would come naturally to her.

Months passed, and Sarah embraced her new outlook. She focused on personal growth, cultivated inner peace, and radiated kindness and acceptance. As she let go of the need to control, she noticed a subtle shift in her relationships. Friends and acquaintances began seeking her guidance, drawn to her gentle wisdom and compassionate presence.

One day, James, the very person Sarah had wanted to help, approached her with a sincere smile. "Sarah, I've been observing your journey and the happiness and peace radiating from you. I've come to seek your guidance in finding my path." Sarah's heart swelled with gratitude. She had come to understand that occasionally, the most profound impact one can make on others is by authentically living their truth without imposing it upon them. She created an environment of trust and openness by respecting their autonomy and allowing them to make their own choices.

From that day forward, Sarah became a guiding light for those who sought her wisdom. She understood that true harmony lies in accepting others' journeys and offering guidance when they genuinely welcome. She nurtured meaningful connections and cultivated a sense of understanding within her community through living and letting live.

Quick Note

The story of Sarah teaches us the importance of living and letting live. Trying to force our ideas onto others can strain relationships and create misunderstandings. We foster harmony and understanding by respecting individual journeys, trusting in the power of personal growth, and allowing others to seek guidance when they are ready.

Chapter 29: Adapting Paths

A determined young woman named Mia lived in a bustling city where dreams intertwined with the hum of ambition. She envisioned her future and meticulously planned her path to success.

As Mia sipped her coffee and reviewed her plans one sunny morning, an unexpected opportunity arose—an enticing promotion at work. Excitement coursed through her veins as she imagined the possibilities that lay ahead. But deep within, a sense of hesitation whispered, urging her to re-evaluate the timing.

Seeking guidance, Mia turned to her mentor, Professor Adams, a seasoned professional known for his wisdom. "Professor Adams, I'm torn. The promotion seems like a golden opportunity, but I worry about the timing and how it might affect my future."

The professor smiled, his eyes reflecting a wealth of experience. "Mia, my dear, it's crucial to assess your current position and consider the potential consequences of your actions. Sometimes, accepting a promotion or pursuing a goal at the wrong time can lead to more trouble than good. Flexibility and adaptability are key."

Mia furrowed her brow, contemplating the professor's words. "But won't postponing or changing a goal make me seem indecisive or less determined?"

Professor Adams chuckled warmly. "Not at all, Mia. Life is a journey of unexpected twists and turns. Flexibility with your goals doesn't diminish your determination; rather, it shows your wisdom in analysing the circumstances and aligning your actions with the best possible outcome."

Intrigued by his perspective, Mia realised the importance of taking a step back and evaluating her situation from a broader perspective. She understood that mindlessly pursuing a goal without considering the timing and potential consequences could lead to unwanted complications.

With newfound clarity, Mia postponed accepting the promotion for the time being. She focused on strengthening her skills and building a stronger foundation, knowing that the right opportunity would present itself when the timing was ideal.

Months passed, and Mia's decision proved wise. Unexpected challenges arose in the company, and the promotion she had initially considered became entangled in the turmoil. Mia found solace in her flexible approach as her colleagues struggled to navigate the uncertain waters. She had avoided the potential pitfalls and started preparing to seize the next opportune moment.

Through this experience, Mia learned that being flexible with her goals didn't equate to giving up or being indecisive. It showcased her adaptability and wisdom in assessing the circumstances. She continued to set ambitious goals, but now with a mindful approach, understanding the importance of aligning them with the right timing.

Quick Note

The story of Mia teaches us the significance of being flexible with our goals. Timing and circumstances play a crucial role in our pursuit of success and mindlessly forging ahead without considering them can lead to unforeseen challenges. By analysing our current position, assessing the potential consequences, and adapting our goals when necessary, we demonstrate wisdom and increase our chances of achieving long-term fulfillment.

Chapter 30: The Ripple Effect

A thoughtful young man named Larid lived in a quaint village nestled amidst rolling hills. He believed in the profound impact of words and actions, understanding that for every action, there is an equal and opposite reaction. This wisdom guided him in navigating life's intricacies, reminding him to consider the consequences before speaking or acting.

One serene morning, as Larid walked along a cobblestone path, deep in contemplation, he noticed his friend Emma sitting alone on a bench. With a gentle smile, he approached her, hoping to offer words of comfort in her time of need.

"Emma, my dear friend, I can see that you're troubled. Is there something on your mind?" Larid asked, his voice filled with empathy.

Emma sighed, her eyes heavy with emotion. "Larid, I appreciate your concern, but I fear the truth might hurt more than it helps. Sometimes, no matter how good our intentions, the timing or the person's readiness to hear certain truths can have adverse effects."

Larid nodded, his gaze thoughtful. "For that, we have to speak wisely, Emma. Our words hold immense power; delivering them without considering the consequences can cause unintended harm. Treating every word with caution is crucial, recognizing that certain truths are most effectively shared when the individual is ready to receive them."

As Emma wiped away a tear, she continued, "Larid, I've seen how you handle situations gracefully and tactfully. Your words have a profound impact because you weigh them carefully. Teach me, my friend, how to choose my words wisely."

Larid smiled, appreciating the trust Emma placed in him. "Emma, it starts with empathy and understanding. Before speaking, put yourself in the other person's shoes. Consider their emotions, readiness, and the potential impact your words may have. Sometimes, silence can be just as powerful, allowing time for wounds to heal and hearts to open."

In the weeks that followed, Emma observed Larid's approach to communication. She noticed how he listened attentively, choosing his words with precision and care. He spoke truthfully, yet his empathy shone through, creating an environment of understanding and acceptance.

Inspired by Larid's example, Emma embarked on her journey of mindful communication. She learned to pause and reflect before speaking, recognizing that her words held the power to uplift or wound. With each interaction, she became more attuned to the consequences of her actions, treating every word with caution and compassion.

Over time, Emma witnessed the ripple effect of her conscious communication. Her relationships blossomed, conflicts diminished, and a sense of harmony permeated her interactions. She realized that by considering the consequences of her words and actions, she could positively impact the lives of those around her.

Quick Note

The story of Larid and Emma teaches us the importance of considering the consequences of our words and actions. Even with good intentions, the timing and readiness of others can significantly impact the outcome. Treating each word with caution and practising empathy allows us to navigate relationships with greater sensitivity, fostering understanding and avoiding unintended harm.

Chapter 31: The Resilient Spirit

In a world filled with sporting fervour, where triumphs and defeats intertwined, there lived a determined athlete named Alex. He had learned through countless setbacks that even when feeling most prepared, there was always a chance of failure. However, he had embraced a powerful mantra: "Never fail to try more."

On a bright summer day, as the stadium roared with anticipation, Alex prepared to compete in a highly anticipated race. With unwavering focus, he dashed forward, leading the pack with remarkable speed. Victory seemed imminent, but fate had a different plan.

Just as Alex approached the finish line, an unexpected stumble caused him to lose footing. Gasps filled the air as he fell, leaving his dreams of triumph shattered instantly. Disappointment and frustration threatened to consume him, but deep within, a flicker of resilience burned.

Days later, Alex found solace in the company of his coach, Coach Roberts. "Coach, I gave it my all, yet I failed to achieve victory. It's disheartening. Should I stop competing?" Alex questioned, his voice tinged with a mix of defeat and determination.

Coach Roberts smiled, a glimmer of admiration in his eyes. "Alex, my dear athlete, failure is an inevitable part of any journey. It is not the fall that defines us but our response to it. You have shown great tenacity and skill, and champions are forged through the adversity of defeat."

Alex contemplated his coach's words, realising the truth they held. "So, Coach, should I continue competing? Will I ever taste victory?"

Coach Roberts placed a hand on Alex's shoulder, offering unwavering support. "Alex, remember that success is not defined by a single outcome but by your unwavering spirit and dedication. Learn from your setbacks, embrace them as opportunities for growth, and work even harder for the next competition. The results will come, eventually."

Inspired by his coach's wisdom, Alex solemnly vowed to pursue victory. He returned to the track with renewed determination, training tirelessly to refine his technique and strengthen his endurance. He embraced each setback as a stepping stone, fuelling his desire to excel.

Months turned into years, and Alex faced victories and defeats in equal measure. But with every race, he grew physically and spiritually stronger. The failures he encountered along the way served as catalysts for improvement, shaping him into a resilient athlete capable of overcoming any obstacle.

And one fateful day, as Alex stood on the podium, clutching the Olympic gold medal that symbolised his triumph, he knew that his perseverance had paid off. The road had been long and arduous, but his unyielding spirit had propelled him forward, leading him to ultimate success.

Quick Note

The tale of Alex enlightens us about the significance of persistence and resilience in the face of failure. Even
114

when feeling prepared, setbacks can occur, but our response to these challenges defines us. By embracing failure, learning from setbacks, and persistently working harder toward our goals, we enhance our chances of achieving success in the long run.

Chapter 32: Creating a Legacy of Innovation

A visionary named Tobias lived in a bustling city where creativity danced through the streets. He possessed an innate understanding of the importance of making oneself necessary and dedicated his life to creating innovative solutions that met people's needs.

Tobias believed that true success lay in the ability to design something others could use and rely upon. He saw the world as a canvas waiting to be transformed through his unique creations. With unwavering determination, he set out to make himself indispensable.

On a radiant morning, while navigating a bustling marketplace, Tobias became acutely aware of a shared predicament: the challenge of accessing clean drinking water. This revelation ignited a concept within him—an innovative device capable of purifying water with remarkable efficiency, ensuring accessibility for all.

Driven by his passion for innovation, Tobias delved into months of research, experimentation, and design. He worked tirelessly, determined to create a solution that would benefit the lives of countless individuals. And finally, his persistence paid off.

With his groundbreaking low-cost water purification device, Tobias approached local communities, demonstrating its capabilities and explaining how it could transform their lives. Word of his invention spread like wildfire, and demand for his creation soon surged.

One day, as Tobias watched families gather around his device, joyfully sipping clean water, a young girl named Rosaline approached him with shining eyes. "Mr. Tobias, thank you for making this incredible invention. It has changed our lives, and we will always be grateful."

Touched by Rosaline's gratitude, Tobias smiled warmly. "Rosaline, my dear, the joy I see in your eyes motivates me. I aim to make myself necessary by creating solutions that meet people's needs. It is through innovation and design that I can contribute to a better world."

As the years passed, Tobias continued to create and innovate, leaving a trail of impactful inventions in his wake. His legacy grew from sustainable energy solutions to life-saving medical devices, and his influence spread far and wide. He had made himself necessary by using his creative genius to address the pressing challenges of his time.

Quick Note

The story of Tobias teaches us the power of making ourselves necessary through innovation and creation. By focusing on designing solutions that meet the needs of others, we can leave a lasting impact and feel a sense of fulfillment. Success comes from using our unique talents to make a positive difference, creating something others can use and rely upon.

Chapter 33: The Power of Positive Thoughts

A young woman named Anastasia lived in the serene countryside, where tranquillity embraced every corner. Through life's experiences, she learned that her thoughts held immense power, shaping her reality and influencing the world around her.

Anastasia believed in the boomerang effect—the notion that what she passed along to others would inevitably return to her. With this in mind, she consciously tried cultivating positive thoughts and spreading kindness wherever she went.

One sunny afternoon, as Anastasia strolled through a bustling park, she noticed a woman sitting on a bench, her face etched with sadness. Anastasia approached her with a warm smile, sensing that she could offer a glimmer of hope.

"Excuse me, may I join you?" Anastasia asked, her voice filled with genuine concern.

The woman nodded, her eyes glistening with tears. "I'm feeling lost and overwhelmed. It seems like there's no light at the end of the tunnel."

Anastasia empathetically listened, her heart reaching out to the woman. "I understand how difficult life can be at times. But I've learned that our thoughts have the power to shape our reality. By focusing on the positive, we invite positivity into our lives."

The woman looked up, curiosity mingling with her sorrow. "But how can I find positivity when everything seems so bleak?"

Anastasia took a deep breath, her voice filled with conviction. "It starts with small steps. Begin by acknowledging the beauty around you—the warmth of the sun, the gentle breeze, and children's laughter. Fill your mind with gratitude for the little blessings, and gradually, you'll notice a shift in your perspective."

Days turned into weeks, and Anastasia's wise words echoed in the woman's mind. With time, she embraced the power of positive thoughts, consciously seeking moments of joy and expressing gratitude for the blessings, no matter how small.

And as the woman's mindset transformed, she noticed a remarkable change in her life. Opportunities appeared where once there seemed none, and kind-hearted individuals crossed her path. The boomerang effect unfolded before her eyes—the positive energy she exuded returned to her in countless ways.

Grateful for Anastasia's guidance, the woman sought her out once more. "Anastasia, you've changed my life. Your words about the boomerang effect were true. As I embraced positivity, it came back to me beautifully."

Anastasia smiled, humbled by the woman's transformation. "Remember, my dear friend, our thoughts are like boomerangs. What we pass along to others has a way of returning to us. By cultivating positive thoughts and spreading kindness, we create a ripple effect of goodness that enriches our lives."

Quick Note

The story of Anastasia teaches us the significance of our thoughts and their impact on our lives. By cultivating positive thoughts and spreading kindness, we create a ripple effect that comes back to us in various ways. Embracing the boomerang effect reminds us to be mindful of our energy in the world, knowing that what we pass along to others will eventually return to us.

Chapter 34: The Power of Words

In a bustling city filled with diverse voices lived a young woman named Amelia. She comprehended the profound influence of words and believed that a person's speech defined them more significantly than the mere absorption of information. Amelia knew how she spoke and said things held the power to create or destroy, and she strived to use her words wisely.

One evening, as Amelia gathered with friends at a local café, their conversation turned toward a recent social issue. Passions flared, and emotions ran high as differing opinions clashed. Amelia, known for her ability to bring calm to stormy conversations, chose her words thoughtfully.

"I understand that we all have different perspectives, and it's important to respect each other's thoughts," Amelia said, calm yet firm. "Let's remember that our words hold immense power. We can use them to build bridges of understanding or to tear them down. Let us choose the former, fostering a healthy exchange of ideas."

Her friends paused, reflecting on Amelia's words. The atmosphere softened, and a renewed sense of empathy emerged. At that moment, Amelia realised the impact of her speech on the group's dynamics.

Days turned into weeks, and Amelia continued to navigate conversations with sensitivity and compassion. She recognised the power of her words to shape the atmosphere, build connections, and inspire positive change. Whether offering encouragement to a struggling friend or engaging in discussions on societal issues, she sought to create rather than destroy.

Amelia's approach to speech extended beyond her social circles. In her professional life, she became known for her ability to communicate effectively, motivating her team and fostering a supportive work environment. She understood that words had the power to uplift, inspire, and encourage growth.

One day, as Amelia reflected on her journey, a friend approached her with gratitude. "Amelia, you've changed the way I view communication. Your mindful approach to speech has transformed our conversations and impacted how I interact with others. Thank you for reminding me of the power of words."

Amelia smiled, grateful for her positive influence on those around her.

Quick Note

The story of Amelia teaches us the profound impact of our words and the power of speech. We are defined more by what comes out of our mouths than what goes in them, as our speech can create or destroy. By choosing our words wisely and speaking with kindness, empathy, and understanding, we can build bridges, inspire positive change, and create a world filled with harmony and positivity.

Chapter 35: Igniting the Journey of Success

A young woman named Abigail lived in a vibrant city teeming with ambitious dreamers. She carried a burning desire to succeed in her personal and professional life. Inspired by the teaching that success begins with a small step, Abigail embarked on her quest for growth and fulfillment.

One fateful day, as Abigail sat at her desk, contemplating the possibilities ahead, a brilliant idea ignited within her mind. With a determined glint, she whispered, "It's time to take a chance and make my dreams a reality."

Armed with courage and determination, Abigail took that small step—she created a detailed business plan outlining her vision, goals, and strategies. Nervously yet firmly, she presented her idea to potential investors, hoping to secure the support she needed to bring her aspirations to fruition.

Uncertainty washed over her as she shared her passion and vision. Doubt crept in, whispering tales of potential failure. However, Abigail reminded herself that success often begins with a leap of faith grounded in a desire to improve.

Days turned into weeks, and Abigail's persistence paid off. A venture capitalist saw the potential in her idea and decided to invest in her vision. With newfound excitement, Abigail took her first steps toward building her business empire.

The path was challenging. Instances arose when obstacles loomed, endangering her progress, and uncertainties resurfaced. However, Abigail drew strength from the teaching that her success was rooted in her small steps, driven by her unwavering desire to improve.

Years passed, and Abigail's business flourished. Her initial small step paved the way for remarkable growth, transforming her life and inspiring others to pursue their dreams. In relationships and personal development, Abigail also applied the same principle, taking small steps toward building meaningful connections and becoming the best version of herself.

One evening, as Abigail reflected on her journey, a friend approached her, eyes brimming with admiration. "Abigail, you are an inspiration. You dared to take a chance and look at the incredible success you've achieved."

Abigail smiled, gratitude filling her heart. "Thank you, my dear friend. I've learned that success always begins with that small step—a leap of faith fuelled by the desire to improve. It's about embracing the unknown and having the courage to chase your dreams."

Inspired by Abigail's story, her friend resolved to take that small step toward her aspirations. And so, the ripple of transformation continued as others discovered the power of that initial leap of faith.

Quick Note

The story of Abigail teaches us the importance of taking small steps toward success. Whether in business, relationships, or life, we ignite our journey of growth and fulfillment through these initial leaps of faith. By embracing the desire to be better and do better and having the courage to take chances, we open doors to remarkable possibilities and pave the way for outstanding achievements.

Chapter 36: The Unending Journey of Learning

A curious heart named Samuel lived in a quaint village nestled amidst rolling hills. He wholeheartedly believed in the teaching that education is never complete, and he approached life with an insatiable hunger for knowledge and growth. Determined to live fully, he embarked on an unending learning journey, prepared to glean lessons from every encounter and experience.

One bright morning, as Samuel strolled through the village, he noticed an elderly man sitting on a bench, engrossed in a book. Intrigued, Samuel approached him with a smile. "Good day, Sir. What fascinating wisdom lies within the pages of your book?"

The elderly man looked up, a twinkle in his eyes. "Ah, young lad, this book is a testament to the unending learning journey. It reminds me that our education is never complete, for there are lessons in every corner of life."

Intrigued by the man's words, Samuel leaned closer, captivated by his wisdom. "But how can one prepare for what life has to teach? How can we be open to its lessons?"

The elderly man nodded, his voice filled with conviction. "Ah, my dear boy, it begins with a mindset— a deep desire to live fully and learn continually. Approach each day with curiosity and a thirst for knowledge. Be present in the moment, allowing yourself to absorb the lessons hidden within even the simplest of experiences."

With newfound inspiration, Samuel embarked on his journey, determined to embrace the teachings of life with an open heart and mind. He sought knowledge from books, engaged in discussions with wise individuals, and immersed himself in diverse experiences that would broaden his horizons.

As the days unfurled into months, and the months seamlessly transitioned into years, Samuel delved deeper into the intricate tapestry of life, unravelling profound truths concealed within. From the gentle whisper of the wind to the vibrant conversations of the marketplace, he found lessons everywhere he turned. Each encounter, whether joyous or challenging, offered an opportunity for growth and understanding.

One evening, as Samuel reflected on his journey, he found himself in the company of a wise sage. "Master, I have dedicated my life to learning and embracing life's lessons. Yet, I still wonder if I am truly prepared for all that life has to teach."

The sage smiled with a pearl of profound wisdom in his eyes. "Samuel, my young seeker of knowledge, the true beauty lies not in being prepared for everything life offers but in remaining open to its teachings. Embrace the unknown, be receptive to the lessons that unfold before you, and trust in your ability to learn and grow. That, my dear friend, is the essence of lifelong education."

Inspired by the sage's words, Samuel continued his quest for knowledge, forever embracing the unending learning journey. He remained open to life's lessons through the highs and lows, triumphs and challenges, knowing that each experience could enrich his understanding and shape his character.

Quick Note

The story of Samuel beautifully illustrates the profound notion that education is an eternal journey, forever unfurling new paths of knowledge and understanding. By remaining open to learning from every experience and embracing the lessons that life has to offer, we continue to grow and expand our awareness. Living with full-hearted dedication involves embracing each day with curiosity, an unquenchable thirst for knowledge, and a mindset that highly esteems perpetual learning.

Chapter 37: The Battle Within

A resilient individual named Eloise lived in a bustling metropolis where dreams and fears intertwined. She understood the power of inner voices and the importance of silencing the voice of fear that often threatened to overpower her. Determined to conquer her doubts, Eloise embarked on a journey to amplify the voices of reason, belief, and confidence within her.

One cloudy afternoon, as Eloise sat on a park bench contemplating her aspirations, the voice of fear crept into her, whispering tales of uncertainty and doubt. Feeling its weight, Eloise took a deep breath and vowed to fortify the other voices in her head.

"I refuse to let fear hold me back," Eloise whispered to herself, her voice brimming with determination. "I will amplify the voices of reason, belief, and confidence until they drown out the voice of fear."

With unyielding resolve, Eloise began her quest. She sought mentors and wise individuals who could offer her

134

guidance and perspective. She immersed herself in books that nurtured growth, inspiring her to embrace her potential and confront her fears.

Days turned into weeks, and Eloise nurtured the voices within her, engaging in affirmations and embracing positive self-talk. Encircled by a supportive network of friends who believed in her, she found their words of encouragement forming a shield against the voice of fear.

One day, as Eloise stood before a daunting challenge, doubts threatened to overwhelm her. However, she had cultivated the voices of reason, belief, and confidence so profoundly that they rose like a chorus within her mind.

"Eloise, summon all that you have achieved," the voice of reason whispered. "You are capable and hold the skills and knowledge to confront this challenge directly." The voice of belief echoed, reflecting the sentiments of those who supported Eloise. "You have surmounted obstacles before and will do so again. Have faith in yourself and the journey you've undertaken."

Lastly, the voice of confidence, bolstered by Eloise's determination, resonated powerfully. "You possess worthiness and capability and deserve success. Stand tall, embrace your inner strength, and conquer this challenge."

With these empowering voices as her guides, Eloise faced her challenge with newfound courage and resilience. The voice of fear, once dominant, dwindled into a mere whisper compared to the harmonious chorus of strength within her.

Months passed, and Eloise's journey of amplifying her inner voice persisted. Through triumphs and setbacks, she realized the power resided within her to control what she allowed to dominate her thoughts. By prioritizing the voices of reason, belief, and confidence, Eloise achieved personal growth and overcame obstacles that once appeared to be insurmountable.

One evening, as Eloise reflected on her transformation, a close friend approached her with admiration. "Eloise, you have become a beacon of strength and inspiration.

Your ability to drown out the voice of fear is truly remarkable."

Eloise smiled, grateful for the journey she had undertaken. Inspired by Eloise's story, her friend resolved to nurture the empowering voices within herself, embarking on her journey of self-discovery and inner strength. Thus, the ripple of transformation continued as others discovered the power of amplifying their voices of strength.

Quick Note

The story of Eloise teaches us the importance of not allowing the voice of fear to overpower our other inner voices. By amplifying the voices of reason, belief, and confidence, we can find the strength to overcome doubts and challenges. We have the ability to choose which voices to nurture and prioritize, ultimately influencing our mindset and propelling us toward our goals.

Chapter 38: The Choice of Heaven or Hell

A man named Leo lived in a quaint village nestled in the countryside. He had faced numerous hardships throughout his life, yet his spirit remained steadfast. One day, a young girl named Daisy approached him as he sat beneath the shade of an old oak tree.

"Leo, why do you always appear so content despite the challenges you encounter?" asked Daisy, her curiosity evident.

Leo smiled warmly and responded, "My dear Daisy, we possess the power to shape our heaven or hell. Life may present us with trials, but how we react determines our experience."

Daisy pondered his words momentarily, her young mind grappling with their significance. "But what about the things we can't control, such as the actions of others or the circumstances we find ourselves in?"

Leo gently nodded and said, "Indeed, there are factors beyond our control. However, even in those moments, we can control our reactions and attitudes. We can choose forgiveness over resentment, kindness over anger, and gratitude over bitterness."

Daisy gazed at Leo, her eyes filled with admiration. "So, you're suggesting that we hold the reins of our destiny?"

Leo nodded and replied, "Exactly. Our thoughts, actions, and choices shape our reality. By embracing this reality, we can turn even the most daunting situations into chances for personal growth and flourishing."

Daisy felt a newfound sense of empowerment as she absorbed Leo's wisdom. She realized that she wielded the key to her happiness and that her choices would chart her path.

From that day forward, Daisy carried Leo's teachings in her heart. She reminded herself of her power to select her response whenever adversity arose. And in doing so, she cultivated her heaven amidst life's trials.

As for Leo, he continued to inspire others with his unwavering belief in the power of personal choice. His legacy served as a reminder that everyone held the key to their happiness and were the architects of their destiny.

Quick Note

The learning lesson from the story of Leo and Daisy is that we have the power to shape our reality and determine our life experiences. We can create heaven even amidst difficult times by consciously choosing positive thoughts, forgiveness, kindness, and gratitude.

Chapter 39: Reputation is Priceless

Once upon a time, a young man named Benjamin lived in the picturesque village of Nestshire. Benjamin was renowned throughout the town for his kind heart, unwavering integrity, and impeccable character. He believed a good reputation was more valuable than any amount of money. He always spoke sincerely, and his actions reflected his genuine concern for others.

One sunny morning, as Benjamin strolled through the village square, he overheard a conversation that captured his attention. A group of merchants had gathered near the fountain, whispering among themselves. Curiosity piqued, and Benjamin approached them with a friendly smile.

"Good morning, gentlemen," Benjamin greeted them. "What seems to be the matter?"

The merchants glanced at one another, hesitating to speak. Finally, one of them, named Theodore, stepped forward. "Benjamin, we're facing a predicament. We've encountered an opportunity to make a significant profit,

141

but it requires compromising our principles. We fear it might tarnish our reputations."

Benjamin listened intently, his brow furrowing with concern. "Tell me more, Theodore. What kind of opportunity are you referring to?"

Theodore sighed and replied, "A wealthy merchant from the neighbouring town wants us to sell him counterfeit goods. The profit we'd make is enormous, but it goes against everything we stand for."

Benjamin understood the gravity of the situation. He gently placed a hand on Theodore's shoulder. "My friend, remember that a good reputation is built upon the foundation of character. It's not worth sacrificing your integrity for temporary gains. Trust that your reputation will care for itself if you do what's right."

Inspired by Benjamin's words, the merchants huddled together, engrossed in conversation. After much contemplation, they reached a unanimous decision. Theodore turned to Benjamin, his face filled with determination.

142

"We've decided, Benjamin. We won't compromise our principles for wealth. Our reputation is worth more than any amount of money."

Benjamin beamed with pride and admiration. "I applaud your decision, Theodore. By staying true to your values, you will inspire others to do the same."

Word of the merchants' unwavering commitment to their reputation spread throughout the village like wildfire. People began flocking to their shops, appreciating the integrity and honesty that emanated from every transaction. Business boomed, and their profits soared.

Meanwhile, Benjamin continued to be a beacon of integrity, offering sage counsel and setting an example for others. His reputation grew even more substantial, extending far beyond the boundaries of Nestshire.

Years passed, and the tale of the virtuous merchants and the wise Benjamin became legendary. Their names became synonymous with trust and reliability, and their businesses flourished.

And so, in the quaint village of Nestshire, the legacy of valuing character above all else was etched into the hearts of its inhabitants. They learned that a good reputation, like a priceless treasure, is built on the foundation of one's character and can never be bought or sold.

Quick Note

The story teaches us that a good reputation is more valuable than material wealth, emphasizing the importance of maintaining character and integrity. By prioritizing our values and doing what is right, we can build a reputation that earns respect and trust from others. Ultimately, our actions and words shape our reputation, and by taking care of our character, our reputation will naturally take care of itself.

Chapter 40: The Courageous Journey

In the rolling hills of Brackenshire, a small village nestled amidst the beauty of nature, lived a young girl named Penelope. She was known for her unwavering determination and indomitable spirit. The village people admired her for embracing challenges, always willing to give her best, and never succumbing to the words "I can't."

One sunny morning, as Penelope roamed the village, she stumbled upon an old, weathered book lying abandoned on a park bench. Intrigued, she picked it up, dusted off its worn cover, and read the title, "The Secret Garden of Possibilities."

Curiosity ignited within her, and she quickly found a comfortable spot beneath a towering oak tree, flipping through the pages of the mysterious book. Words of wisdom and inspiration filled each page, but it was one passage that caught her attention:

"You never really lose until you stop trying. Instead of saying, 'I can't ever accomplish anything,' saying 'I'll try,' on the other hand, can perform wonders. Until you try, you don't know what you can do."

The words resonated deeply within Penelope's heart, stirring newfound courage within her. Determined to put these teachings into practice, she set off on a quest that would test her abilities and push the boundaries of her potential.

Her first challenge awaited her at the foot of the village's tallest hill, aptly named "Mount Perseverance." Towering over the landscape, it seemed like an insurmountable obstacle. Yet, fuelled by the belief that she could achieve the impossible, Penelope took her first step.

Penelope climbed higher with every laboured breath and aching muscle, refusing to give in to the doubts that whispered in her mind. She repeated the words from the book like a mantra, "I'll try, I'll try."

A crowd gathered as she neared the peak, witnessing her remarkable determination. They marvelled at her unwavering spirit, inspired by her refusal to accept defeat. With one final surge of strength, Penelope triumphantly reached the summit, tears of joy streaming down her face.

From that day forward, the people of Brackenshire spoke of Penelope's incredible feat. Her story spread far and wide, inspiring others to embrace the power of perseverance. Penelope became a beacon of hope, reminding everyone that they never genuinely lose until they stop trying.

Buoyed by her success, Penelope embraced new challenges, fearlessly tackling each one with the words "I'll try." She discovered hidden talents and strengths she never knew existed through her determination and refusal to give up.

The legacy of Penelope's courageous journey is a testament to the transformative power of trying. The village of Brackenshire learned that by banishing the words "I can't" and embracing the phrase "I'll try," they could unlock endless possibilities and embark on extraordinary adventures.

And so, in the enchanting village of Brackenshire, the spirit of resilience and the pursuit of dreams became intertwined with the very essence of its inhabitants. They learned they held the key to their success and happiness and only genuinely lost once they stopped trying.

Quick Note

The story beautifully illustrates that the power of trying and refusing to give up is essential for personal growth and success. It highlights that the words "I can't" limit our potential, while the phrase "I'll try" opens doors to endless possibilities. The story encourages us to embrace challenges with determination, as we never lose until we stop trying, and through perseverance, we discover our hidden strengths and achieve remarkable feats.

Chapter 41: The Generosity Game

A young woman named Audrey lived in the bustling city of Greenwood. She possessed a heart filled with kindness and believed that the accurate measure of success lay not in how much one received but in how much one gave. Audrey understood that by giving generously, she could create a life abundant with joy and fulfillment.

One sunny morning, Audrey spotted a peculiar flyer that caught her attention. It announced the "Generosity Game," a city-wide challenge where participants were encouraged to give as much as possible to others. The flyer promised that the rewards would far exceed any material possessions.

Intrigued by the concept, Audrey decided to embark on this unique adventure. She eagerly signed up for the Generosity Game and received a small card with instructions. The card read, "Your challenge is to find three opportunities to give selflessly within the next 24 hours."

Determined to make a difference, Audrey set out on her mission. Her first opportunity arose when she noticed an elderly gentleman struggling to carry groceries. Without hesitation, she rushed to his aid, offering a helping hand. The gratitude that radiated from his eyes was worth more than any reward.

Audrey continued her quest and stumbled upon a local park where children played. Their laughter filled the air, but she noticed their worn-out soccer ball barely holding together. Realizing they deserved a proper ball for their games, Audrey rushed to the nearest sports store.

Audrey approached the store owner with a warm smile, explaining the situation. Touched by her kindness, the owner generously donated a brand-new soccer ball for the children. Audrey's heart swelled with happiness, knowing that her giving would bring the young players joy.

With only one opportunity left, Audrey pondered where her final act of generosity would take her. Just as she was deep in thought, she stumbled upon a homeless shelter.

A thought crossed her mind—these individuals deserved warmth and comfort. Inspired, Audrey organized a clothing drive within the community, encouraging everyone to donate their gently used clothes.

The response from the community was overwhelming. People lined up, eager to contribute to the cause. Together, they gathered many clothes, blankets, and essential items to donate to the shelter. Audrey stood in awe, witnessing the power of collective giving and its impact on those in need.

As the 24-hour challenge drew to an end, Audrey reflected on her experiences. She realized that the real reward of the Generosity Game was not the accolades or material gains but the profound sense of fulfillment and the connections she forged with others.

Word of Audrey's selfless acts spread throughout the city, inspiring countless others to embrace the spirit of giving. The community came alive with acts of kindness, and the once-strangers united to create an abundant life through generosity.

Audrey's journey taught her that success is measured not by the number of possessions accumulated but by the impact she made in the lives of others. She discovered she received far more in return by giving more—a wealth of love, gratitude, and a sense of purpose that money could never buy.

Quick Note

The story conveys a powerful message that true success and abundance come from giving selflessly to others rather than focusing solely on personal gain. By genuinely embracing a mindset of generosity and actively looking for chances to help others, we can shape a more prosperous life in meaning and satisfaction. The story shows the strength of coming together to do kind deeds. When we collaborate as a team to give and support, we can bring about a meaningful and positive change in the lives of others. This wonderful dynamic helps cultivate a community where compassion and abundance flourish.

Chapter 42: Rule Your Mind

A young woman named Eliza lived in a quaint village nestled amidst rolling hills. She possessed a bright mind and unwavering determination to create a fulfilling life. However, self-doubt and negative thoughts threatened to consume her journey.

One day, as Eliza sat under the shade of a towering oak tree, she pondered her wise grandfather's teachings. "Rule your mind, my dear," her grandfather had often advised, "Choose your thoughts wisely and watch how they shape your reality."

Inspired by her grandfather's words, Eliza embarked on a quest to master her mind. She realized that every morning presented a new opportunity to decide the course of her thoughts. Determined to take control, she started her days with affirmations of positivity and gratitude.

However, Eliza soon realized that winning the battle within took effort. Negativity and doubt would creep into her mind, attempting to undermine her progress.

Yet, she persevered, determined to overcome these obstacles.

Eliza would remind herself in moments of doubt, "I am the ruler of my mind. I have the power to choose my thoughts and create a positive reality." With each small victory over negative thinking, her confidence grew, and her world transformed.

Eliza noticed a shift in her external circumstances as she took charge of her mind. Opportunities manifested effortlessly, and relationships became more fulfilling. She discovered that ruling her mind meant ruling her world.

While strolling through the village one day, Eliza overheard villagers discussing their struggles and limitations. Empathy filled her heart, and she deeply desired to share her newfound wisdom. Gathering the villagers, she spoke with conviction, "Friends, we possess the power to shape our lives through the thoughts we entertain. Rule your mind, and you will rule your world."

The villagers listened intently, inspired by Eliza's words. They realized their minds held the key to their happiness and success. Encouraged by Eliza's example, they, too, embarked on the journey of self-mastery, eager to create positive change in their lives.

From that day forward, Eliza became a guiding light in the village, reminding everyone of the power within. By ruling their minds, the villagers embraced a life filled with hope, optimism, and limitless possibilities.

Quick Note

The story of Eliza teaches us that the choice to rule our minds lies within our grasp. We can shape and align any reality with our aspirations by consciously steering our thoughts away from negativity and doubt. Each day presents an opportunity to reclaim our power and create a world of positivity and fulfillment.

Chapter 43: The Humble Hero

A man named Mark resided in a bustling city known for its towering buildings and busy streets. He possessed exceptional skills and earned celebration as a hero due to his remarkable abilities. However, amidst the admiration, Mark remained grounded and humble, understanding the true essence of his greatness.

One sunny afternoon, a young admirer approached Mark with wide-eyed wonder as he walked through the city. "Mr. Mark, how did you become such a remarkable hero?" the young boy inquired.

Mark warmly smiled and replied, "Being a hero isn't solely about my skills, young one. Humility guides my actions and keeps me open to learning."

The boy's eyes sparked with curiosity. "Why is humility so important, Mr. Mark?"

Mark paused, gathering his thoughts. "Humility helps us recognize that we're never fully complete, that there's always room to grow and improve. It keeps us grounded amidst success and reminds us to remain approachable."

The boy nodded, captivated by Mark's wisdom. "But, Mr. Mark, aren't heroes supposed to exude confidence and strength?"

Mark chuckled softly. "Confidence and strength are indeed crucial, my young friend. Yet, genuine greatness resides in balancing confidence and humility. It involves understanding that we can continually refine our skills, and every encounter presents an opportunity to learn from others."

Continuing their walk, Mark shared tales of his journey toward humility. He recounted instances when pride had overshadowed his abilities and how those experiences had imparted valuable lessons.

"Remember, young one," Mark said, placing a hand on the boy's shoulder, "Remaining teachable, no matter how much you already know, marks a true hero. It enables us to embrace new perspectives and evolve as individuals and leaders."

The boy thoughtfully nodded, absorbing Mark's words. He realized humility wasn't a weakness but a strength propelling heroes forward. From that day on, he committed to nurturing humility in his journey, embracing continuous learning and growth.

Mark sensed he had conveyed a priceless lesson as he bid the boy farewell. Humility wasn't reserved solely for heroes; it was a quality uplifting every individual on their path to greatness.

In the years ahead, the boy would emerge as a hero in his own right. And, like Mark, he would carry humility's torch, inspiring others to embrace teachability and strive for greatness.

Humility gave birth to true heroes whose greatness shone brilliantly, grounded in the awareness of perpetual learning and achievement.

Quick Note

Mark's tale underscores that authentic greatness walks hand in hand with humility. It serves as a reminder that welcoming learning and adopting a teachable mindset are vital for personal enhancement. By reigning in our egos and embracing humility, we can become protagonists of our stories, inspiring others on the journey.

Chapter 44: The Triumph of Resilience

In a small town lived a young and ambitious entrepreneur named Evelyn. She had always dreamed of starting a business and making a name for herself. With unwavering determination, she launched her online clothing store, 'Elegance Boutique.'

However, the initial months were fraught with numerous setbacks. The store struggled to attract customers, and Evelyn faced financial challenges. Despite her best efforts, the business teetered on the brink of failure.

Feeling disheartened, Evelyn sat alone in her dimly lit office one evening, contemplating her next move. She recalled the wise words she had once read: "Defeat isn't bitter if you're smart enough not to swallow it." This sentiment struck a chord within her, igniting a spark of resilience.

Refusing to let failure define her, Evelyn decided to shift her perspective. She began viewing setbacks as valuable lessons and opportunities for growth rather than as signs of defeat. She delved into extensive research, studying successful entrepreneurs and learning from their failures.

With newfound determination, Evelyn implemented a strategic marketing plan, revamped her online store, and concentrated on providing exceptional customer service. She harnessed social media platforms to engage with her target audience, seeking their feedback and addressing their concerns.

Months elapsed, and gradually but steadily, Evelyn started to witness the positive effects of her efforts. Her customer base expanded, and the once-struggling 'Elegance Boutique' became a thriving online fashion destination.

Evelyn received an unexpected email as she prepared to open her store one sunny morning. It was an invitation to showcase her collection at a renowned fashion event—an opportunity that would propel her brand to new heights. Overwhelmed with joy, Evelyn realized her journey was worth it.

Reflecting on her experience, Evelyn comprehended that failure was simply a stepping stone to success. It was her resilience, her refusal to let defeat consume her, that propelled her forward. She had embraced the truth that setbacks were not the end but an integral part of the journey.

From that day forward, Evelyn embraced challenges with an unwavering spirit. She understood that success was not a destination but a continuous process of learning and growth. And with each setback she encountered, she reminded herself, "Defeat isn't bitter if you're smart enough not to swallow it."

Quick Note

Evelyn's story teaches us that failure is not an ultimate endpoint but an essential part of the journey toward success. By rejecting the notion of defeat defining her and welcoming setbacks as chances for growth, Evelyn transformed her struggling business into a flourishing venture. Her tenacity and determination remind us that setbacks should be treated as valuable lessons, propelling us toward our aspirations.

Chapter 45: The Power of Forgiveness

A woman named Alice lived in a small town nestled by the coast. She had faced her fair share of challenges and disappointments throughout her life, but one incident had left a lasting mark on her heart. The betrayal of a close friend had left her bitter and resentful, carrying the weight of anger and hurt for far too long.

One sunny day, as Alice strolled along the beach, lost in her thoughts, she stumbled upon a young boy named Daniel. He seemed lost and on the verge of tears. Curiosity overcame her, and she approached him with a gentle smile.

"Are you okay, young man?" she asked kindly.

Daniel hesitated, but the sincerity in Alice's eyes convinced him to open up. He shared how his best friend had broken his trust, leaving him feeling betrayed and hurt.

Alice listened attentively, her painful memories resurfacing. She knew all too well the heavy burden of holding onto grudges. Drawing from her own experience, she decided to impart a valuable lesson to Daniel.

"You see, Daniel," she began, "forgiveness is a powerful tool. It may seem difficult, but it can free both the giver and the receiver from bitterness and resentment."

Daniel looked puzzled, but his curiosity urged him to ask, "But how can forgiveness benefit both people?"

Alice smiled warmly, reminiscing about her journey. "When we harbour anger and refuse to forgive, it burdens us emotionally. It consumes our thoughts, saps our energy, and prevents us from moving forward. By forgiving, we release ourselves from this burden and create space for healing and personal growth."

She continued, "Forgiveness also grants the person who hurt us the opportunity to learn and grow. It allows them to recognize their mistakes and, perhaps, make amends. It's a chance for both parties to find peace and move forward."

Daniel contemplated Alice's words, his young mind grappling with forgiveness. After a moment of silence, he nodded slowly.

"You're right, Alice. Holding onto anger won't change what happened. It will only make me feel worse. I want to be free from this burden."

With relief, Alice knew she had planted a seed of understanding and growth within Daniel. As they walked along the shore, their conversation continued, focusing on the importance of forgiveness and the strength it takes to let go.

From that day forward, Alice and Daniel forged a deep bond, supporting each other on their journeys toward forgiveness and personal success. Through their shared experiences, they discovered that forgiveness was not a sign of weakness but rather an act of courage and wisdom.

And so, Alice's story serves as a reminder that by choosing forgiveness over grudges, we lighten our load and create a pathway to a brighter, more fulfilling future.

166

Quick Note

The story teaches us that forgiveness is a powerful tool that benefits both the giver and the receiver. Holding onto grudges and grievances only weighs us down and hinders our personal growth. Choosing forgiveness allows us to let go of the past, find inner peace, and create space for healing and positive change.

Chapter 46: Building Blocks of Success

Once upon a time, a determined young woman named Nora lived in a quaint village nestled amidst rolling hills. She understood that preparation was not merely a step toward success but the building block upon which it stood. Nora's unwavering belief in the power of preparation set her on a remarkable journey toward achieving her dreams.

From an early age, Nora recognized the importance of being well-prepared. Whether for school exams, sports competitions, or personal projects, she approached every task with a meticulous plan and a steadfast commitment to readiness. She knew that success demanded a solid foundation of thorough preparation.

Nora's dedication to preparation became even more evident as the years passed. She pursued higher education, acquiring knowledge and skills to shape her future. She sought mentors and experts in her field, absorbing their wisdom and guidance. Nora forged

168

herself into an undeniable force by practising and refining for countless hours.

One day, an opportunity of a lifetime presented itself to Nora. A renowned company, impressed by her reputation for thorough preparation, offered her a chance to lead a ground-breaking project. The challenge was immense, but Nora embraced it with confidence. She knew her practice had equipped her with the tools needed to succeed.

In the weeks leading up to the project, Nora immersed herself in research, analysis, and strategic planning. She left no stone unturned, anticipating every obstacle and devising contingencies. The depth of her preparation instilled a sense of calm amidst the storm, allowing her to navigate challenges with resilience and adaptability.

When the time came to present her project to the company's executives, Nora stood before them, poised and well-prepared. She flawlessly articulated her ideas, backed by comprehensive data and a clear vision. Her thorough preparation paid off, impressing the executives and earning their trust and admiration.

Nora's project became a resounding success, propelling her career to new heights. The impact of her preparation reverberated throughout her life, shaping her professional achievements and personal growth. Her unwavering commitment to practice inspired others, proving it was the cornerstone of success.

Quick Note

The story of Nora reminds us of the vital role that preparation plays in achieving success. Through her unwavering commitment to thorough preparation, Nora demonstrated its transformative power. The story inspires us to recognize preparation as a vital stepping stone toward our goals, empowering us to face challenges and make the most of opportunities with confidence and readiness.

Chapter 47: The Power of Perception

S ophie, a young woman passionate about psychology, was captivated by the notion that our thoughts wield the ability to mould our reality. She immersed herself in the study of perception and the potency of the mind. One day, strolling through a bustling city, she observed individuals hurrying past one another, their countenances awash with stress and worry.

Intrigued, Sophie resolved to put her knowledge to the test. She embarked on a social experiment, approaching strangers with a smile and a cheerful salutation. To her surprise, the responses exhibited significant variance. Specific individuals appeared taken aback, whereas others reciprocated her warm greeting.

As Sophie continued her experiment, she encountered Tom, a man seated alone on a bench, absorbed in contemplation. Sensing an opportunity, she approached him and initiated a conversation. Their dialogue delved into the might of perception and our thoughts' role in shaping our reality.

A staunch believer that life existed beyond his control, Tom openly shared his tribulations and frustrations. He believed he was a victim of circumstance, lacking control over his destiny. Sophie tactfully challenged his viewpoint, urging him to consider the prospect that his thoughts wielded a more substantial influence than he recognized.

With time, Sophie and Tom persisted in their discussions, delving into conscious creation. Sophie recounted anecdotes of individuals who had metamorphosed their lives through positive thinking and deliberate actions. Tom's curiosity burgeoned, prompting him to interrogate his pessimistic convictions.

One day, as they sat on the same bench where their initial encounter had occurred, Tom gazed at Sophie and confided, "You know, I've devoted an extensive amount of time fixating on what's beyond my control, inadvertently neglecting the potency within me. I yearn to transmute my reality and fashion a life of joy and purpose."

Bolstered by Tom's newfound resolve, Sophie assumed his mentor role, aiding him in reshaping his mindset and concentrating on affirmative assertions. They toiled in tandem, establishing objectives and envisioning the life Tom aspired to attain. Gradually, he began perceiving minor shifts in his circumstances, bolstering his determination to persevere.

Months later, Tom stood before an audience, recounting his tale of metamorphosis. He underscored the significance of assuming responsibility for one's thoughts and deeds, highlighting how a perceptual shift had ushered him into novel prospects and a sensation of empowerment.

Elevated by her impact on Tom's life, Sophie apprehended the profound integrity of the tenet she had perpetually upheld.

Quick Note

The omnipotence of our thoughts and perceptions is staggering, steering the reality we encounter. By conscientiously opting for affirmative thoughts, we can magnetize more positive experiences. Assuming command of our thoughts and proactively labouring to realign our mindset can pave the way for revolutionary change and a life of purpose and felicity.

Chapter 48: Mindset Matters

Amidst the vibrant city of Veridian, Matthias, a budding artist, and Aria, an aspiring musician, set forth on a quest to pursue their dreams. Along their path, they encountered numerous obstacles that tested their determination.

One evening, Aria voiced her frustration as they sat on a park bench, gazing over the city lights. "Matthias, it feels like the world is opposing us. Rejections and setbacks greet us at every corner. How can we maintain a positive outlook amidst all these challenges?"

Matthias looked at Aria, his eyes emanating calm determination. "Aria, we possess the power to shape our reality," he said. "True, we confront hardships, but how we react truly counts. Our thoughts, actions, and beliefs can potentially mould our experiences."

Aria listened attentively, a glimmer of hope illuminating her eyes. "But what about the circumstances beyond our control?" she inquired. "How can we surpass those?"

Matthias warmly smiled and responded, "Though we can't govern every twist of fate, we can govern our attitude and mindset. We retain the capacity to perceive obstacles as gateways to growth and transformation. We can forge our destiny by focusing on our sphere of influence and taking proactive strides toward our objectives."

Empowered by Matthias's words, Aria experienced a revitalized sense of purpose. They pursued their artistic endeavours with unyielding resilience. Each rejection fuelled their determination, and every setback became a stepping stone toward their aspirations.

With time, Matthias and Aria's unshakable faith in their ability to shape reality bore fruit. Their artistic prowess flourished, and opportunities materialized. They attracted kindred spirits who championed their dreams and shared their creative vision.

One evening, as they stood on an imposing stage, Matthias and Aria surveyed the audience, brimming with gratitude. Aria turned to Matthias and whispered, "We did it. Despite the challenges, we crafted our reality."

Matthias nodded, a glint of pride in his eyes. "Indeed, Aria. Our journey educated us that our thoughts and actions mould our destiny. By embracing our creative power, we transformed obstacles into milestones on the path to our dreams."

Unified, Matthias and Aria persisted in inspiring others with their narrative. They reminded each heart they encountered that they harboured the potency within to shape their reality. Through their art and unwavering conviction, they motivated others to embrace their creative odysseys and manifest their envisioned lives.

Henceforth, Matthias and Aria's legacy endured, a tribute to the transformative potential of embracing one's power to shape reality.

Quick Note

Matthias and Aria's tale teaches that we wield the authority to mould our reality via our thoughts, actions, and beliefs. They instruct us that our response and mindset determine our fate, even when facing challenges and uncontrollable circumstances. By embracing our creative capacity, we can metamorphose hindrances into stepping stones toward our aspirations, materializing the life we envision.

Chapter 49: The Poison of Envy

In a tranquil seaside town, a young woman named Amelia lived. She possessed numerous commendable traits that adorned her character, but with time, envy stealthily infiltrated her heart, tarnishing her thoughts and actions. One day, while traversing the bustling market, she couldn't suppress the urge to compare herself to those in her vicinity.

Amelia's confidant, Benjamin, discerned the shift in her demeanour and became apprehensive. He approached her, his eyes reflecting concern. "Amelia, I've noticed you've been distant lately. Is something troubling you?"

Amelia released a sigh, and her gaze veiled in discontent. "Benjamin, I can't escape this sensation of envy toward others. It seems like everyone possesses something I yearn for—a superior job, a caring relationship, or material possessions. It's gnawing at me."

Benjamin listened intently, perceiving the corrosive nature of envy. "Amelia, I've understood that envy is a relentless force. It not only erodes your happiness but also impedes your growth potential. It blinds us to our blessings and deprives us of gratitude."

Amelia nodded, her countenance a blend of remorse and desire. "But how can I liberate myself from this toxic cycle? I feel entangled in this perpetual comparison."

Benjamin rested a reassuring hand on her shoulder, his voice tender yet resolute. "The journey commences with a shift in perspective, Amelia. Rather than fixating on others' possessions, cultivate a sense of gratitude for what you already possess. Commend their achievements without diminishing your self-worth."

Amelia inhaled deeply, absorbing the wisdom in Benjamin's words. "You're right, Benjamin. Envy is only causing me harm. I'm determined to release its grip and embrace a more enriching existence."

Brimming with resolve, Amelia embarked on a voyage of introspection and appreciation. Each day, she tallied her blessings and celebrated her triumphs, no matter how minor. As she nurtured genuine gratitude for her life's facets, the weight of envy started to dissipate.

With time, Amelia unearthed the potency of contentment and self-acceptance. She realized that others' possessions didn't dictate her value, but her unique journey did. By relinquishing envy's hold, she cleared the path for joy, serenity, and personal maturation.

As Amelia's metamorphosis unfurled, her relationships deepened, and her accomplishments burgeoned. Her positive aura and genuine happiness attracted others. Her story proved that envy consumes itself, and true fulfillment is found by embracing one's path with gratitude and contentment.

Henceforth, Amelia persisted in inspiring others, underscoring that the expedition toward genuine happiness commences by liberating oneself from envy and embracing the abundance that already thrives within one's life.

Quick Note

This narrative underscores that comparing ourselves to others and surrendering to envy merely ushers in discontentment and hampers our advancement. By nurturing profound gratitude for our blessings and wholeheartedly celebrating others' achievements without belittling our own, we can unshackle ourselves from envy's toxic loop, fostering a profound emotional transformation. Welcoming contentment and self-acceptance unlock the door to genuine joy, enabling us to value the unique odyssey of our lives.

Chapter 50: The Power of Gratitude

In the quaint town of Oakville, a woman named Amyra lived. She possessed a radiant spirit and an unwavering belief in the power of gratitude. As the sun's first rays painted the sky every morning, Amyra would sit in her garden, embracing nature's beauty.

One day, her neighbour, Mrs. Thompson, approached her with a puzzled look. "Amyra, I've noticed that no matter your challenges, you always seem positive. How do you do it?"

Amyra smiled warmly and replied, "My dear Mrs. Thompson, the practice of gratitude fills my heart with true power. Each day, I focus on the blessings surrounding me, no matter how big or small."

Mrs. Thompson seemed intrigued. "But Amyra, how can being grateful give you power?"

Amyra gently took Mrs. Thompson's hand and led her to a nearby rose bush. "You see, Mrs. Thompson, when we express gratitude, we shift our perspective. We notice the abundance in our lives, and in turn, we attract more blessings. Gratitude is the key that unlocks the door to our inner strength and power."

Mrs. Thompson pondered Amyra's words, her mind racing with possibilities. "So, by being grateful, we tap into a source of strength and power within us?"

Amyra nodded and said, "Exactly, my dear friend. Gratitude tenderly unfurls our hearts and minds to embrace the present moment, allowing us to cherish life's simple joys and draw strength from even the most trying times. This transformative practice allows us to navigate life's twists and turns gracefully."

Mrs. Thompson felt inspired by Amyra's wisdom and resolved to cultivate gratitude in her own life. She noticed the little blessings she had overlooked before— the laughter of her grandchildren, the warmth of a cup of tea, the beauty of a blooming flower. With each act of gratitude, she felt her inner power growing.

As time passed, Amyra's Garden became a sanctuary of gratitude, attracting people from all walks of life.

Together, they shared stories of gratitude and celebrated the power it had brought into their lives.

And so, Amyra's teachings and the transformative power of gratitude forever changed the town of Oakville. People learned that true strength and power lie not in material possessions or external circumstances but within the depths of a grateful heart.

Amyra's legacy lived on from that day forward, reminding everyone that gratitude could ignite a powerful transformation.

Quick Note

The tale of Amyra teaches us that gratitude is a wellspring of genuine power. By nurturing a heart brimming with gratitude and concentrating on our blessings, we can access inner fortitude and draw positivity into our lives. The practice of gratitude equips us to navigate challenges while skillfully finding delight in the present moment.

Thank You

Hey there, you made it to the end—cheers to that!

I'm so glad we got to share this journey. I hope it left you with fresh insights, a little inspiration, and a new way of seeing the small moments that matter. If you enjoyed the read, I'd love it if you left a quick review. Just a few words can go a long way in helping me create more stories—the kind that help you notice the little things or guide you toward the beauty of life.

Scan Me

>> Leave a Review on Amazon<<

Thanks for being a part of this. Seriously, you're the best!

About the Author

Sati Siroda is an inspirational author passionate about empowering young minds through storytelling. With a knack for weaving simple yet profound tales, Sati inspires readers to embrace their unique potential and navigate life with courage and purpose.

Sati's diverse academic journey—from engineering to education, business, and communication—combined with her extensive travels and time spent in various countries for education, business, and skill development shapes her holistic storytelling approach. Her experience teaching in schools and universities has further enriched her understanding of young minds, helping her find her path as a storyteller who connects deeply with her audience. Her multifaceted background enables her to connect with readers in relatable and innovative ways.

Her stories are fueled by a belief in the transformative power of narrative. Drawing from her expertise in strategic communication and her love for literature, Sati crafts engaging, uplifting books that instill resilience, emotional intelligence, and self-confidence in her readers. Her mission is clear: to inspire the next generation to dream fearlessly, think critically, and approach life's challenges with creativity and optimism.

Through her heartfelt stories, Sati creates a world where every page becomes a stepping stone toward growth, and every character serves as a guiding light. She warmly invites readers of all ages to embark on a journey of self-love, self-discovery, and empowerment through the enchantment of her books.

Stay connected with Sati Siroda on Instagram: *@SatiSiroda.*

Made in the USA
Middletown, DE
19 April 2025